THE TAO OF CONTEMPLATION

D0967168

THE TAO OF CONTEMPLATION

*re-sourcing
the inner life*

JASMIN LEE CORI

SAMUEL WEISER, INC.

York Beach, Maine

First published in 2000 by
Samuel Weiser, Inc.
P.O. Box 612
York Beach, ME 03910-0612
www.weiserbooks.com

Library of Congress Cataloging-in-Publication Data
Cori, Jasmin Lee.
    The Tao of contemplation: re-sourcing the inner life / Jasmin Lee Cori.
        p. cm.
    Includes bibliographical references and index.
    ISBN 1-57863-131-9 (alk. paper)
    1. Spiritual life   2. Contemplation.   3. Taoism.   I. Title
BL624 .C6655 2000
291.4'35—dc21   99–058156

MG
Typeset in 10.5/13 Weiss.
Cover design by Kathryn Sky-Peck

Printed in the United States of America
07 06 05 04 03 02 01 00
8 7 6 5 4 3 2 1

Contents

contents

contents

contents

Preface

I began writing this book because it is what opened up when I became quiet. It is what met me in the silence. I gave myself over and followed the flow. When I later started talking to people about what I was up to, I was met by a number of questions. Why a book about contemplation? Why is this important now? And what can you, personally, tell me about it that will help me in my life? Here are some of my answers.

Our lives are out of balance. Our culture as a whole is consumed with outer life. We spend almost all of our time chasing after success and recognition, love and security. We are so used to looking for satisfactions outside ourselves that we even go shopping for spiritual experiences. We don't realize that if we stop chasing and become still, we will find within ourselves riches beyond what we dreamed possible.

Contemplation is a counterbalance because it slows us down and sends us back inside ourselves. It is a path of stillness where the teacher is to be found within. We need this right now. It is a corrective to our tendency to look outside for answers and to give away our spiritual authority. It is a corrective to our busy lives. Without silence, we cannot touch the deepest parts of ourselves; without silence, we cannot know God.

This simple, gentle path, if followed sincerely, can be a road home. It can also lead to lifestyle choices that have a harmonizing effect in themselves. It can help us find a middle way that honors both emptiness and fullness, both restraint and enjoyment.

preface

This book is for people who want to find a simpler, quieter, more spacious way to live, people for whom the outer life is not enough, who hunger for the richness and meaning that comes from being in contact with the mysteries. I write for the many travelers on the spiritual journey, wherever they may be. I try to speak about deeper experiences in ways that are accessible and can be understood without a lot of background or training. It is vitally important to me to go beyond simple psychology and a friendly brand of universalist spirituality, into the more frightening and challenging aspects of spiritual life.

At its core, contemplative life is about losing yourself. It is about being erased, annihilated. It is not usually helpful to state this in such stark terms, for then we are bound to defend ourselves. No one wants to be annihilated. Yet there is grace in annihilation. There is more to gain than there is to lose. What we lose is the container of the small self, and what we gain is our more fundamental identity with the ground, the oneness, God. We are annihilated by love.

Although I think we can create a secular version of contemplative life that is quite pleasant in itself, if we really open ourselves in the silence, the depth will call us. The depth is our own true nature. We cannot help but open into what we fundamentally *are* once we stop maintaining our smaller identity. So, although this book is written with a Taoist flavor that is more gentle than forceful, more accepting than urgent, it is still about a path of liberation.

I write about contemplation from a unique perspective. I am not a recognized contemplative, nor do I come out of one of the great contemplative traditions. I am a renegade in this field, a person who has had to find her own way. I don't agree with those authorities who say that a contemplative life requires a rigorous structured practice and a teacher. I think spirit is more creative than that. It has been said that there are as many ways to lead a spiritual life as there are people. I think this is true of the contemplative life as well. The form is not important. What is important is that you cultivate those qualities that character-ize the contemplative life.

I have always been drawn to the inner life. There is no adventure I find more fascinating than the adventure of Being, the mystery of who we are. I devote my life to this with great joy and all of the usual resistance. I am a mystic in the sense that many of us are: I have tasted the sweetness of the divine, delighted in the ecstasy of oneness.

I am contemplative by nature in that I need a certain amount of quiet and simplicity. I prefer an uncluttered life. Over the years, I have come to know and appreciate emptiness, something that can be quite threatening at first. It takes time to relax into emptiness and recognize it for the doorway that it is. One of my friends said that I lead the most contemplative life of anyone she knows, yet I had never defined it in this way. Her comment helped me see that such a life can take many forms. It will look different for everybody.

This book is an attempt to build a bridge between secular and spiritual life, which ultimately means dissolving the division between the two. This extends the topic beyond my central metaphor for contemplation (waiting in silence with empty hands) to include some more active processes for cultivating the inner life. We cultivate the inner life so that we can have access to something beyond ourselves. To understand more about the relationship between the individual and the collective, the most inward and the boundless, let's turn to Ira Progoff's book, *The Well and the Cathedral.*

preface

Progoff, creator of the Intensive Journal Process, employs a beautiful metaphor of going down one's inner well and encountering the underground stream. Since this extended metaphor, created as a meditative text, so powerfully describes the process of contemplation, I will end this preface by sharing it in some detail.

Many of Progoff's images, like those of ancient Taoist writers, center around nature. Progoff actually opens his first verse with the words of Lao Tse:

> *Muddy water,*
> *Let stand*
> *Becomes clear.*[1]

How simply Lao Tse says it! Six short words, a Taoist treatise on contemplation. Stillness leads to clarity. What is not said is that the clarity helps us perceive our deeper nature and is a characteristic of that nature. We are that clarity.

Becoming still and quiet is the condition for entering the stillpoint that opens yet further in the metaphor.

> *The center point relaxes.*
> *It loosens,*
> *Stretches, opens.*
> *The center point*
> *Becomes the shaft of the well*
> *Within our Self.*
> *It is opening wider;*
> *Its walls are softening,*

---

1. Ira Progoff, *The Well and the Cathedral* (New York: Dialogue House Library, 1977), p. 35.

preface

The shaft within us is opening,
Making space so we can move
Further down the well
Into the depth of our Self. [2]

Notice the images. The walls soften, causing an inner shaft to open. This opening allows us to go deeper. This is not just poetic language. It describes the process as precisely as the more technical descriptions presented by other authors. Progoff continues.

Each time as we go deeper
The Atmosphere softens to us.
It becomes more comfortable,
More congenial.
It absorbs us more warmly.
We know
We belong here. [3]

In this passage, Progoff is not only saying that we grow more comfortable with the depths, but hints of the responsiveness of the depth to us. The depth absorbs us, welcoming us home.

When we pass through the depth of the well, we come to the underground stream. It is the transpersonal beyond the personal, the collective energies beyond the separate self. Here is where I differ with Progoff. I don't believe that the underground stream is beyond the well; I believe it is actually the depth of the well. The well is a partitioning of the stream, just as the ego-self is a partitioning of Being. Ultimately, they are the same.

---

2. Ira Progoff, *The Well and the Cathedral*, p. 91.
3. Ira Progoff, *The Well and the Cathedral*, p. 103.

Progoff acknowledges the stream as the source of the well and describes it as drawing us through the dark silence. Here is the contemplative thread again. We are drawn through the silence. It is stillness that allows us to feel the persistent and subtle pull into the underground stream where we intermingle freely, letting go of individual identity. This is an important idea, although, once more, I would describe it a little differently. I think it is the letting go of individual identity that allows us to enter the stream. When we let go of separation, we feel the whole.

Progoff describes how many before us have gone through their individual well to absorb and be absorbed by this underground stream. Upon their return, they placed a stone at the base of the well. In time, these stones made a beautiful cathedral where many came to pray. I think we can see this as the process by which many religions have developed. The mystic returns from his absorption in the divine and tries to create markers that can show others the way. The problem is, as Progoff notes, that the cathedral now covers the well. Religion replaces contemplation, and we lose our access point.

It is the access that I am writing about. In a sentence, the purpose of this book is to help you enter the silence so that you may be drawn through the inner well to the joyful abundance of the underground stream.

Acknowledgments

No one creates alone. I wish to thank my teachers and friends, too many to name, for their love and encouragement. Special thanks to Gabrielle Rebacas and to Carol Layton for their enthusiastic support of me as a writer. Thanks, too, to those who provided feedback early in the process, especially Gail Bishop and Julie Webster, and to Elaine Upton for her encouragement to bring in more of my own story and "put the wrinkles back in." I am also indebted to my friend and fellow explorer, Julisa Adams, whose dialogue with me has become part of this book.

A Note on Language

Words are funny things. They are like the finger pointing to the moon; they are useful in showing us where to look, but the words themselves are a long way from the reality they point to. This leaves us with the paradox that for language to point effectively, it must be as precise as possible; yet to get to the truth, we must go beyond discriminating concepts and open our intuitive channels. Metaphor and poetry can help us with this, and so I use them. I have tried to make my writing precise enough to satisfy the intellect, and metaphoric enough to stimulate the imagination. It is opening up the experiential field that will bring the real harvest.

Besides poetry and metaphor there are other ways my language may sometimes appear imprecise. For example, I move back and forth in a rather casual manner between the various names used to refer to ultimate reality. Sometimes I use the word *God*, sometimes *Tao*. You may substitute whatever word works most effectively for you. My intention is to create an open, friendly tone that is inclusive. In keeping with this, I often use the pronoun *we* as I work my way through the narrative, recognizing that not every person may fit a particular description. Enough of us do, though, that it is not out of hand. After all, we're all in this together.

Introduction

There is nothing esoteric about contemplative life. It is a simple
bloom not frequently found in the climate of contemporary
Western culture. We have been too busy to cultivate the silence,
simplicity, and emptiness necessary to reach the fullness of
mystical life. And yet the path is not as inaccessible as we may
first imagine.

We can all live a more contemplative life. There is not one
way, but many ways. We can start wherever we are and let a
more contemplative lifestyle evolve naturally, as an expression
of certain aspects of our being. Contemplation is the stillness
and coolness of a quiet mind, the openness of a surrendered
heart, the simplicity of just being ourselves. It is the balance of
not too tight and not too loose.

We will open more eagerly to contemplative life if we
recognize it as something that is rich and juicy. If we see it as
only stern and dry, those with a joyful heart will not be drawn
to it. What a relief to discover that we don't have to behave like
monks! There is room to monkey around a little. True nature is
not grim.

The Tao of Contemplation takes the essence of contemplative
life (the elements of silence, solitude, simplicity, surrender,
receptivity, and an orientation toward direct encounter with the
one reality) and combines them with the naturalness, spontaneity, and joy of a Taoist approach. I find them to be perfect
partners.

introduction

The book straddles East and West, shuttling back and forth between the language of theistic and nontheistic systems, finding the differences totally unimportant to the true posture of contemplation. Explorations throughout the text help readers integrate and embody the material. A few, like the one on Open Presence (see page 75), can be used as practices.

The book is sequenced in a way that reflects the process of inner work. The more practical issues are placed up front, and the deepest parts are saved for the end. The first two chapters describe the context and approach of the book. They begin to build a definition of contemplation and its place in spiritual and personal growth. In the first chapter, I differentiate between two journeys: one to find ourselves and one to lose ourselves. I try to show how these two journeys relate and how contemplation figures into each of them. The second chapter describes the more intuitive and individual approach to contemplation that I call "the natural way."

The next four chapters describe how to create the elements of a contemplative lifestyle. Chapter 3 discusses the need to create empty space in your life, and chapter 4 presents the issues involved in returning to a simpler way of living. Chapter 5 describes the balance between restraint and enjoyment, the much championed "Middle Way." In chapter 6, this balance is applied to relationships, finding that both solitude and intimacy have an important place in spiritual life.

Just as the first star comes out when it is dark enough to see it, our deeper self comes into range when we are quiet enough, clear enough, and sensitive enough to perceive it. The next three chapters address this. Chapter 7 describes the many ways in which people can cultivate a state of inner quiet. Chapter 8 develops the theme of receptivity, and chapter 9 explores the central quality of openness.

introduction

In chapter 10, I come back to the concept of the two journeys and the importance of working on the personality. I introduce a method for staying with one's immediate experience that is a useful tool in both psychological and spiritual work. Chapter 11 discusses letting go and chapter 12 explores the deepest surrender of all—letting go of the separate self. This leads into the last two chapters which are devoted to the mystical side of spiritual life. Chapter 13 focuses on the importance of love. The book ends (chapter 14) with the jewels of the night—the great treasure of mystical union and the other precious experiences that happen on the way to this union. There is no question: contemplative life is rich indeed.

I don't think there will ever be a definitive text on how to create a lifestyle that allows for more contact with spirit. There are too many different ways to achieve it. It is my hope that *The Tao of Contemplation* will support you in moving toward the depths in a way that is natural to you.

Listen, the silence is calling.

chapter 1

The Inner Life

If you want to be rich
stop chasing after the things of the world.
Go inside.
What you will find will stop you dead
and you will want no more.

This is the essence of most, if not all, spiritual teachings. The real riches lie in the kingdom within, yet many people live their whole lives not knowing how to find them. Their energies are absorbed in the outer world, keeping up with the demands of a busy life. The only inner life they know is really the inside lining of the outer life, for it consists almost entirely of their emotional and mental involvement with the world around them.

There is another inner life. We may enter it through this surface layer, but it goes far, far beyond that. It is concerned, not so much with the ups and downs of our personal lives, but with our deeper relationships with life and spirit. It is concerned with an inner nature that is the ground of everything.

Although culture at large does not support this inner life, there is growing interest in it. The marketplace is booming with books, classes, and workshops, all appealing to this hunger for a more genuine, free, actualized life. While there is much that we can learn from these sources, we must remember that real freedom is not something that anyone can sell us. We cannot purchase enlightenment, any more than our ancestors could purchase salvation. We need to learn how to re-source our inner life by once more making our way to the source of it.

It is a long journey with many paths, some straight and narrow, others circular and inclusive. If you want the straight and narrow path, I suggest you find a spiritual teacher and make this your life. For most of us, that won't work. We take what may look like (and be) a longer route, but the changes we make are broad and sweeping. We're not necessarily in a hurry. The goal is not just to get enlightened, but to self-actualize as well.

TWO JOURNEYS

In a sense, there are two journeys: one to find ourselves and one to lose ourselves. Of course it is not that simple. At different levels, the truth looks different. That is why the teachings of sages like Ramana Maharshi at times sound contradictory. Many of Ramana's teachings are a record of his responses to questions asked by various seekers. His answers were tailored to the individual needs and consciousness of the questioner. Just as the view from the mountain looks different from different vantage points, so too the view of reality varies according to our level of consciousness.

This is why the relationship between these two journeys is so difficult to describe. Some would say that they are really one journey, and they would be correct. Others claiming the same thing would not be correct because they would mean something quite different by it. Because I think there is more harm right now in equating the two processes than in differentiating them, I am emphasizing the distinction.

Many of today's popular books on spiritual growth deal more with finding yourself and expanding that self than with the ruthless task of losing yourself. Self-actualization, which can be defined as fulfilling all of one's unique human potential, becomes confused with Self-Realization, defined as knowing your true identity as the more universal Self. Actually, I don't

like using the word "self" in this context because it is so intri-
cately wed in most of our minds with the sense of individual
identity. When we are talking about the transpersonal ground of
being that is our true nature, we might better describe it as the
"suchness," the "beingness," the "isness" that constitutes everything. It is a far cry from the individual self, which, because of
our identification with it, keeps us from knowing this larger Self.
To keep this dinstinction clear, I will always capitalize the word
"self" when referring to this deeper, broader experience.

The journey to find ourselves (the first journey) is the
process of individuation. When we realize what this really
involves, we see that it is a journey very few people complete.
Few break free from the conditioning of the past to fully and
completely express their unique being. So it is fitting that much
of our collective attention, as well as the fields of psychology
and personal growth, are concerned with shepherding people
through this process.

Much of what I say about contemplative life can be applied
to this first journey. Making space to be with yourself, examin-
ing the issue of identity, becoming more open and present,
learning to tolerate stillness and to let go of control—all of
these are useful to the process of becoming a more authentic
person.

They are also useful in the process of losing ourselves (the
second journey). By becoming more open and more present, for
example, we come into deeper contact with the larger Being,
which allows us to recognize that we are not the identity we
carry around inside our heads. This helps us let go of that
identity and know that we are not truly separate from the larger
unity, which is exactly what the second journey is about. In a
similar fashion, learning to tolerate stillness not only helps us
face ourselves more squarely (the first journey), but takes us

beyond the activity of the ego. Without that activity, the ego falls away (the second journey). So the same process serves both ends, depending on how deeply we pursue it.

It may be said that both journeys culminate in knowing who we really are, yet they do not point to the same thing. In the first journey, what we discover is the authentic person, without mask or self-limitation. In the second journey, we learn that any such identity is still only a part of the picture. It is still the outer skin. In the second journey, we discover that we are something much more eternal and mysterious, something that can change into almost any form and still be true to itself. It is hard for our minds to grasp an identity that is independent of the particulars in this way. It helps if we can let go of our minds a little bit and try to feel from our bodies and our hearts.

The first journey is familiar to us. In many ways, it is a self-improvement project. We can use our usual motivations and strategies to get behind it. The second journey, in contrast, is a radical departure. We must let go of almost everything we know, every familiar way of being. It represents a complete metamorphosis. There is a paradox here: as radical as this second journey is, it can lead to an outer life that looks totally ordinary.

In many Buddhist teachings, we hear the idea that after enlightenment, all that is left is chopping wood and carrying water. We don't disappear into the ethers, but return to the chores of daily life more embodied. We come into our bodies and sensations in a way that allows us to really experience them. The commentary—the story we impose on life—is gone, and what is left is simply what is.

To some people, this seems to imply that the experience of pure sensation is the totality of spiritual life. This is not how I experience it. When I am in deeper states, I sometimes feel a fine presence that pervades everything. I am in contact with vast dimensions inside of me—or which I enter by going inside. Sometimes, it is hard to tell what is inside and what is outside, or which world is more real, although I see that the outer world is but an expression of this invisible reality. When chopping wood and carrying water, I can be present to the wood and the water, to my hands and my feet, and I can also be present to the formless essence that makes the universe sing.

THE ROUTE HOME

The two journeys contain many roads. The journey to find ourselves includes personal growth work, psychotherapy, education, relationships, parenting, career, interests, spiritual community, and much more. Often, it follows the shape of our lives. The first journey is broad and inclusive.

The second journey is not. It whittles us down rather than builds us up. We lose structure rather than gain it. In the second journey, it doesn't really matter what you do for a living, how fulfilling your relationships are, or what temple you pray in. It doesn't matter what you wear. (In the first journey, there can be a lot of experimentation with personal style and appearance.) The second journey strips us of all that. In some sense, we are stripped of our individuality—or what we have taken to be our individuality. We give up many of the outer distinctions, not because they are bad and should be extinguished, but because they are not our true being. This is not to suggest that our true being is some homogeneous mush in which everyone is the same. There is a uniqueness that the mind cannot anticipate and that can only be known when we come upon it in our inner travels.

What is this reducing diet? What can whittle us away like this? Hard spiritual work. This doesn't necessarily mean twelve hours on a meditation cushion with a Zen master whacking you on the back. It doesn't require a guru who throws your ego onto the ground and humiliates you. It doesn't necessarily come with years of selfless service. Any of these may be part of your path, but there are gentler ways as well.

What I am describing in this book is an entrance ramp to a contemplative lifestyle that can fit into the modern world, that honors individual differences, and that is true to the natural intelligence that is operating through the universe and in each person who knows how to get out of the way and listen. Contemplation is about listening. It is not about ordering God around, not about creating rituals to manifest our desires, not about secret formulas for spiritual transformation. Contemplation is the yin of spiritual life. It is the receptive side of things.

Thus it is not about controlling, but about giving up control; not about knowing, but about entering the way of unknowing; not about getting more, but about giving up everything that stands between you and the no-thing-ness of your true nature. The mystical way of expressing this is to say that the contemplative life is about giving yourself to the Beloved, about surrendering everything between you and God.

Such terms are stark and demanding, and I don't want to scare people. When you feel mystical passion, you want to give everything; before this, you may just want a quieter life, to recognize the spiritual in the commonplace, to find solace in silence. It is enough.

THE FRUITS OF CONTEMPLATIVE LIFE

Contemplative life is not a starvation diet. A bounty of fruits lines the path all along the way. One of the first of these fruits is the sense of spaciousness that comes when we stop filling all of our time. Because we are not racing about, we have a sense of more leisure. We slow down and smell the flowers. As we break free of our conditioning and listen to our own rhythms, we enjoy a sense of harmony and flow. We feel more balanced because we are not run by the requirements of outer life alone, but have also begun to cultivate an inner life. We come back to ourselves. What a relief! We step out of the haze of our thoughts and come into the moment. In a word, we become "present."

From this sense of presence, along with a growing sense of connection, comes the feeling of more meaning and, at the same time, less need to articulate what that meaning is. We are not living for something that is down the road. The meaning is right here, in the moment.

Unresolved feelings may rise to the surface as we sit and face ourselves, but we know that this is the road to peace. We are no longer running away. We are here, facing the good and the bad, learning to hold it all.

These are juicy fruits, rewards enough for our changes. But they are not all. As we deepen into the second journey, we find an even more abundant harvest. Most of these fruits come as we release the small self. It is like stepping out of a tin suit, free at last to be and move without constraint. A whole new dimension of being opens up inside of us. We come home, our hearts overflowing with gratitude. The fruits of our own essential nature are more wondrous and delectable than we could have hoped—the sweetness of our own nature and the sweetness of divine nature, one luscious ecstasy.

Am I exaggerating? Not at all. The language may seem flowery, but the riches are far greater than even the most superlative descriptors. I don't mean to imply that contemplative life is all some kind of honeyed bliss. There are deserts to cross, times of great aridity and discouragement, times when we are terrified. But the fruits most certainly are there, and the fruits are real. They liberate in us a love that transforms us, giving us new eyes through which we view the world. Here is a poem about this experience.

New Eyes

Running through the village
embracing everyone she meets,
she laughs in ecstasy.
People call her *mad.*

"New eyes!" she cries.
"I have been given new eyes!"
And it is true.
For the scales which had previously blinded her
are gone now, erased
revealing such utter glory
that her mind took flight,
leaving only a rapturous heart
in an old, weathered body
racing through the streets
on fire with love.[1]

---

1. Jasmin Cori, *Freefall to the Beloved: Mystical Poetry for God's Lovers* (Boulder, CO: Golden Reed, 1996), p. 111.

chapter 2

Contemplation— the Natural Way

Drop what is imposed.
Find the way that is natural to you.
Your own flow is in harmony with the Tao.

Contemplation is very important in spiritual life. Really it is the center, although it is possible to be involved in religious rituals and belief systems without it. It may not always be called by the same name, but it has the same root. Contemplation is reaching beneath the clatter of the mind to abide in silence and there encounter something.

Those who believe in a god, seek silence to meet that god. In the nontheistic traditions, like Buddhism, there isn't a divine being; there is simply *being*, the nature of reality. While this may look like a significant difference, there is more common ground than may first be seen. As our contemplation deepens, we go beyond the imagery of our beliefs to the direct perception of *what is*. We are taken beyond the god made in our human image to a reality that defies images. Thus the differences between the various wisdom traditions appear on a level that is later transcended—the level of mind. In Taoist philosophy, it is said that the Tao that can be named is not the real Tao.

A TAOIST TWIST

There are two schools of Taoist thought. Religious Taoism is based largely on an attempt to achieve immortality through various physical practices and religious rites. Philosophical

Taoism (called Contemplative Taoism by one author) is based largely on the Tao Te Ching, the writings of the legendary Lao Tzu, which were expounded and popularized by the later Chinese philosopher Chuang Tzu, who lived in the fourth century B.C. This school of Taoist thought has a great deal to teach us about living a harmonious and balanced life. It is this branch of Taoism that concerns us here.

The most common translation of the word *Tao* is "the way." More than anything else, it is the *natural* way, for there is no fixed path in this philosophy. Prescribed forms cannot stay true to the fluid nature of reality (also called the Tao). Only centered, spontaneous action can be in harmony with this ever-changing flow.

One means used by the early Taoists to come back to "the way of things" was to cultivate stillness and inner quiet. This is the essence of contemplation. Without the interference of mind and emotion, awareness becomes clear. Only in this empty, clear awareness, can we sidestep all that we impose upon reality and come to know "things as they are." To live in harmony with the Tao thus means living in harmony with the inner nature of things. This inner nature is not pinched or restrained, but an abundant, joyful streaming. A Taoist approach is, therefore, never ascetic.

The path is one of balance: the inward is balanced with the outward, stillness is balanced with action. Contemplative life doesn't need to be monochromatic; it can have variety, plenitude. We can be in the world in a concrete and real way. This is the opposite of many of our ideas about contemplative life. How much better it is to allow the ideas to change rather than try to lop off parts of ourselves to conform to an ideal. Ideals are always partial and therefore not true to life. We must let go of them if we are to find our own way.

THE NATURAL WAY

There is no mold for the natural life. It is a matter of living in harmony with our own nature. It may seem contradictory for me to speak of each of us as having an inner nature when I suggest elsewhere that our true nature is the underlying ground, which is an undivided whole. Yet this is the magic of creation: the one becomes the many. Each manifestation emphasizes different qualities and expresses them in its own way. Just as each snow-flake is unique, each person is a unique manifestation of an underlying consciousness.

This diversity is an inherent part of the physical world. Unfortunately, we have interfered with this natural variety and created an artificial homogeneity. We see this in the loss of plant varieties, species, and options for human living. Whenever we try to limit life to any one way, we are going against the Tao. There is not one way; there are an infinite variety of ways. The Taoist relishes the differences.

I am suggesting that, for each of us, there is a way of being that is more natural than any other way. To find it, we must look inside. It is there, as surely as the tree is in the acorn. The way is not so much a blueprint as an unfoldment that is true to an inner nature. It is both true to this inner nature and responsive to the moment. It is the natural expression of one's being in the present circumstances. Thus the life that is natural for me, living on the crest of the 21st century, is different than it would be if I were living in the Middle Ages. Yet in all cases, independent of gender and race and all the other particulars, there is a life that is true to the essence of me.

My approach is to invite you to develop the qualities central to contemplative life and let the forms appear on their own. I am not giving a prescription or formula, but rather outlining what may be called the natural *way* ("tao") of contemplation.

FEELING OUR WAY ALONG

To follow what feels natural requires a certain independence from how others believe things should be done. We must be free and open in the moment, sensitive to the situation. When we think we already know how things should be, we stop listening. To stay open to the truth in each moment, we must question the truths handed down to us and the truths we knew yesterday. Life becomes a constant inquiry in which we feel our way along. We feel the texture of the moment, feel which way things are headed.

We are feeling for the flow of reality and where it is taking us. This requires a great deal of discernment. Going with the flow is not simply going wherever the winds of personality and social conditioning blow us. It is not following every impulse, but rather feeling into each impulse to ascertain where it is coming from. We need to be able to sit through much of what propels our actions and feel for the deeper impulse, the sacred impulse that leads to true unfoldment.

This process is very intuitive and very individual. It requires a great deal of work and a loyalty and precision, which is quite different from the popular notion that creating your own path allows you to be a bit lazy. Of course, there are also potential downfalls in working in an individual way. Critics say it is too easy to create a package of beliefs and practices that comfort us rather than serve as a crucible for transformation, too easy to delude ourselves and take the easy way out. They say we need a structure to provide focus, and we need the inner teachings and grace that come with being part of a long-standing tradition. There is some truth here.

I think it is wise, at least for a while, to be part of a group that follows a reliable, alive spiritual teaching. It can help guide you through passages that are precarious and difficult to navigate alone. The support of others is a powerful boon. I know that when I gave myself to a particular path for ten years, I developed in ways that I could not have otherwise. And yet I came to a place where I needed to leave the security of that path in order to stay true to my own calling. Rabbi Rami Shapiro calls this "leaving home." He said true spirituality demands that we leave everything we know to wander without a goal, path, teacher, or teaching. Buddha, Mohammed, Lao Tzu, and Jesus all "left home."[1]

Of course, it is nice to have a home so that you can mature and someday leave it, but I can't even say that this is required. Nor would I go quite so far as to say that you must some day leave your tradition. These are decisions you have to make for yourself as your process unfolds. I suggest that if you have a tradition that works for you, you stay with it as long as it is useful. On the other hand, if you've never found a place to call home, it will be your task to make a home, at least for yourself.

Being eclectic doesn't mean that you can't go deep. Just because someone has moved from one teaching to another, or has commitments to several different teachings simultaneously, it doesn't mean that person is approaching spiritual life in a superficial way. There is a difference between a casual, ever-changing collection of rituals and beliefs and a commitment to deep inner work, a difference between being a dilettante and a creative pioneer.

Ultimately, authentic spiritual growth comes from within. It is nurtured by the environment, but the changes are changes within us and must come through us. We can't get there on

---

1. Mark Matousek, ed., "Should You Design Your Own Religion?" *Utne Reader*, July–August, 1998, p. 47.

borrowed wisdom or borrowed grace. This doesn't mean our truth needs to be different from everybody else's. It simply means that it must be truly ours. We must know it through our own experience. The critical question is whether being part of a tradition supports and opens up our experience or whether it puts us to sleep.

TRUE TO THE ESSENCE

The truth is not always easy to recognize. Listening for the voice of guidance, we often get deluded by our own unconscious masquerading as something it is not. We may think we're hearing from angels, or entities, or our higher self when really it is some part of the ego slipping in with its own agenda. Recently, I heard the story of a young girl struggling to put herself through college whose "heart" directed her to buy a new $24,000 car. This seems a little suspicious to me, as do the many messages people seem to be getting about having a special mission. Who wouldn't like to have a special mission? Who wouldn't like to hear that the person we are so infatuated with is the partner we'll end up with? We must take up the challenging task of learning to discern when it is the truth we're feeling and when it is wishful thinking.

This is one example of a part of spiritual life where discernment is terribly important. Every experience involves an interpretation of some kind, because it is coming through a perceiver and the perceiver is not a blank slate. Remembering the subjective nature of what happens to us may help us avoid making too much out of our spiritual experiences. Not only do we face the danger of distortion and self-deception, but the ego tends to become bloated on such experiences. It uses them to puff itself up, just as it uses accomplishments in other realms. This is what Tibetan Buddhist teacher Chögyam Trungpa calls *spiritual materialism*—an acquiring (materialistic) attitude transported to spiritual life.[2]

There is a second kind of spiritual materialism that also poses a danger. It is mistaking the form for the formless, the packaging for the gift. This is a hazard inherent in most, if not all, spiritual methods. It comes, not from the forms themselves, but from our way of relating to them.

Twenty years ago I heard a story that I have always remembered. It was about a person who experienced an awakening while sitting under a tree eating an avocado. When he returned to the village and told the people about his experience, he was disappointed with their response. They wanted to know which tree and what kind of avocado. Fixated on the incidentals, they missed the important point.

This is a natural tendency of the human ego, which is oriented to what is observable and what we can control and manipulate. We take this attitude into our spiritual training schools and think that if we can just be on the right path and do it the right way, we can get what we're after. We become caught in the surface aspects, attached to the phenomena associated with the path—whether that be rituals, robes, states of enlightenment, sacred scriptures, or teachers. When this happens, we are trapped by the trappings.

To stay true to the deeper truth, we must discriminate between the inner essence of a teaching and its surface features, between genuine expressions and imitations. We must know the difference between true silence and a gag rule, between solitude and isolation, between self-punishing renunciation and intelli-

---

2. Chögyam Trungpa, *Cutting Through Spiritual Materialism* (Boston: Shambhala, 1987).

gent restraint. I put a lot of emphasis on this issue of learning to discriminate and feel for the truth because it is the fastest way I know of to reach the depths. Since the truth is *what is,* then feeling for and following the truth always harmonizes us with the way things are and takes us deeper into reality.

Feeling for the truth is also a great counterbalance to whimsy. It is what makes the "natural way" that I describe here a path of liberation rather than simply an enjoyable way to live.

chapter 3
Clearing the Space

Nowhere to go
Nothing to do
Nobody to be
I am myself.

It takes time and space to settle into the depth of our being. It is here that we come to know, not only the authentic person, but what in some traditions is called the True Self. It is deeper than the personality, independent of time, the place where we intersect with the divine.

The problem is that we are often caught on the surface with an abundance of places to go and things to do. Most people's lives today are severely over-scheduled, leaving little room for spontaneity or quiet. Those who do have "time on their hands" often seem at a loss about what to do with it. Time becomes a burden, relieved only by the little diversions that substitute for living. Most of us have yet to learn the subtle art of being.

CREATING OPEN SPACE

In order to have a more contemplative lifestyle, we need to clear some space. I am speaking of a lifestyle conducive to what I call the natural way of contemplation. The lives of monks (the "professional contemplatives") are often highly regimented. The natural way, in contrast, isn't based on an imposed order. We seek and abide in silence in our own time and our own ways. If we are to do this spontaneously, we must break old habits and come back to the natural rhythms of body and soul.

We start by creating open space in our lives. It is the space to simply *be*, where there are no images to maintain, no things we need to do. Although we all love to have free time to pursue our interests and hobbies, what is most valuable about open space is the opportunity to come into deeper contact with ourselves. Open space in our lives helps us relax into the openness of being.

One way to create open space is to give yourself what I call "flow time." Flow time is unstructured time where you just let the day unfold without planning it. It is really very enjoyable and, contrary to your fears, it may not mean the end of productivity, but rather be a new way of getting done what needs to be done (and setting aside what doesn't). There may be some distortions at first, but these should straighten themselves out if you hold an intention to really listen for what is right in the moment. I find that my unconscious is much better at scheduling me than any management system I can think of. It takes all the variables into account, even those my conscious mind is unaware of. In flow time, you learn to surrender to the flow of your own inherent rhythms and the larger flow of which you are a part. Practicing this can become a way of life.

If this is new to you, I suggest you start with part of a day when you aren't working. At each juncture, simply ask what is in the flow right now. It may be washing the dishes or it might involve something you never think about. When you don't know what's next, stop and wait until something feels natural. It will soon become obvious, and there you are, flowing again.

After a while, you may get spoiled and not want to be squeezed into a schedule again. Life without open space begins to feel a little dry.

LETTING GO OF STRUCTURE

To outsiders, it may look as if I lead a very undisciplined life because there is almost no external structure to it. Sometimes I work in the morning, sometimes in the evening, sometimes all day long, and sometimes not at all. A Monday doesn't necessarily look any different from a Saturday. I don't have set meal times or even a set number of meals each day. The only apparent structure is that I am usually awake during the day and asleep at night.

A life like this can be chaotic, or it can have a tremendous amount of discipline. I am referring here to the discipline of listening carefully for whatever is in the flow, staying true, not to a schedule, but to an inner prompting. It is the discipline of not getting lost in distractions, the discipline of not filling your life with television or social obligations, of learning the balance between hoarding your time for what you hold dear and being free enough to try new things and be gracious with others.

We can become very possessive of our time. For years, it was one of my deepest attachments. Then the structure of my life changed, and I found it relaxing not to have to monitor my time so tightly. It allowed for much more flow. I still have that pushing part of me that tries to make me feel guilty when I've been unproductive for very long. Not wanting to be controlled by this, I challenge it. I try to look objectively. Is this just an instance of my inner critic being uncomfortable, or am I failing to live up to something more real? Who is running the show?

I remember thinking about this one day as I was hiking up a mountain. I had no idea when I woke up that morning that I would be hiking, but that is what naturally unfolded. I was just following the flow, as was my habit. How far can I go with this way of living, I wondered. Am I really following a deeper flow, or am I just being bandied about by my unconscious? What am I trusting? Then this funny thought came into my head: Perhaps there is a cosmic joke where I am about to leap off a cliff, wondering if I can trust God to catch me. God laughs and asks, "Who do you think carried you up here?"

We each have different needs for structure, and they may vary at different times. Some people do best with a lot of structure. We all benefit from having certain things we can count on. The structure of a stable relationship, family, or organization can provide the "holding" we need to grow. The task is to determine which structures are helpful and which are not. Does the structure provide the support and consistency that allows us to be vulnerable and creative? Does it transform chaotic activity into something more harmonious? Or does the structure put us to sleep?

Learning to live with less structure is really learning to live with more spontaneity and openness. Ultimately, this is a good thing. Life is unpredictable, and we need to be able to adjust to rapid changes. It is also good practice for the second journey, where our inner structures break down. This can be quite frightening. I remember feeling one evening as if a giant scaffolding inside me had suddenly collapsed. Yet what surprised me was that it didn't hurt anything. The scaffolding fell, but the cathedral still stood, majestic and unharmed. The collapse of my mental structures did not touch my true, essential nature.

I will describe the structure of the self in chapter 12. It is the loss of this structure that leads to the expansive, open nature of unity consciousness.

Taking Time for Renewal

Our productivity-driven culture doesn't allow nearly enough time for renewal. We have forgotten the wisdom of letting the field lie fallow. We need times of rest, for example, at the end of a long program of education or after many years in a career. Actually, we need times of renewal in both the large and small cycles of our lives. We need sabbaticals and Sabbaths and moments in the day when we stop "doing" and refresh ourselves.

I know a woman whose work could be fairly relaxing, but her ambition to succeed drives her to work ever-longer hours, trying desperately to jump the next economic hoop. Increasingly, she lives for vacations. It takes her at least a week to wind down, and her vacations are becoming longer and more expensive. This fuels the need to work yet longer hours. She is caught in a vicious cycle with too little time for rest.

I have often thought that I would like to live in such a way that I don't need vacations. I would still like to be able to take them if I want, but I don't want to need them. I was, therefore, interested when I recently read an article by spiritual teacher Eknath Easwaran, who said he hadn't taken a vacation in over a third of a century.[1] Now in his late 80s, Easwaran says he doesn't need a vacation because he gets so much joy from his life of service. I would also expect that his meditation practice and his contact with the deeper dimensions give him all the time and space he needs.

I am not implying that such practices can create more clock hours, but rather suggesting that we can drop into spaces where we are no longer in clock time. When the fast and feverish activity of the ego stops, in a sense, *we* stop. The chain of memories collapses and we are here in the eternal now.

This doesn't happen when we carry our concerns around with us. I was hiking on a mountain trail recently and saw a man

---

1. Eknath Easwaran, "The Power of Faith," *Blue Mountain: A Journal for Spiritual Living*, January 1998, vol.9, #1, p. 5.

talking on a cell phone. His attention was far away from the sounds of the crickets and the soft breeze blowing through the pine boughs. I have been equally far away just carrying on conversations in my head. The refreshment comes when we can drop all of that. When you are not caught in the thousand details of a too-full life, even a half hour walk can feel very spacious.

When we reconnect with our natural flow, we create rhythms in our lives that can sustain us. We can learn to balance activity with rest, work with play. We learn how much time we need alone and the kind of time we need with others. For me, it also means that time indoors is balanced with time outdoors. Nature feeds my soul.

It also helps if we can stop and enjoy little moments during the day. I love watching the last fifteen minutes of light before the sun sets. To steep myself in this light fills and renews me. I get the same satisfaction watching the changing blue of the evening sky or certain kinds of weather. Some people like to take a moment to simply breathe or smile or look at something beautiful. Taking a moment to feel grateful also helps bring a sense of richness and appreciation to life. Many have found inspiration in the simple practices that the Buddhist monk Thich Nhat Hanh describes in his writings.

HONORING THE EMPTY SPACES

Talking about times of renewal brings us to a discussion of the Sabbath. In his book, *Holiness*, Donald Nicholl describes the Sabbath as the time to be still and rejoice in the presence of God.[2] Nicholl believes it is important to keep the appointed

---

2. Donald Nicholl, *Holiness* (New York: Seabury Press, 1981), p. 78

Sabbath time; otherwise we will find excuses to continue whatever activities we are engaged in or believe to be important. In following the Sabbath discipline, we give up the notion that it is our time to do with as we please. It is not our time; it is God's time.

I think there is merit to this argument. Yet, not being part of a tradition that honors the Sabbath in this way, my Taoist nature wants to let this time to be still and rejoice follow its own natural rhythms. My Sabbath is therefore unplanned and, some might argue, not a real Sabbath. Yet it does require fidelity. I must stop whatever I am doing whenever I feel my essence calling me. I must set down my work or play, not just at one appointed time each week, but at unexpected intervals. The danger, of course, is in not having the attunement necessary to do this.

We need space in our lives, not just to open ourselves to the presence of God (the religious context), but to open up to ourselves. In his book, *Meditations*, best-selling author Thomas Moore speaks of our need for empty spaces. Just as a loaf of bread needs air in order to rise, we need empty spaces in our lives, times when we can withdraw from the world.[3] It is the counterpoint to entering fully into life.

My secular version of this is a practice I call "doing nothing." I first learned it years ago when I would lay in my "womb room" with candlelight and music and simply stare into space. It was time to sink into me and be with all the things that were going on there. It was also the precursor to learning how to dwell in emptiness, but that came later. During those early

---

3. Thomas Moore, *Meditations: On the Monk Who Dwells in Daily Life* (New York: HarperCollins, 1994), p. 4.

years, I was mostly learning to be with my internal world. I had to let go of my habitual "doing" long enough to find out who I was. Lao Tzu understood this when he wrote, "Muddy water / let stand / becomes clear."

Ironically, I don't "do nothing" as much as I used to. Maybe the process has served its purpose and become more integrated into my life. It is less important to mark off time for stillness if you can hold some of that stillness within you as you go about your daily activities. At any rate, I do recommend it— especially if it sounds a little unsettling. I suggest you give yourself two hours a week to begin. Be aware: Your appetite for this may grow!

My idea of a contemplative life lived the natural way is that it has plenty of open space and empty space. It has times when we listen for the next thing to do, times for spiritual practice, and times that we purposefully do not fill. It does not have more structure than is useful, but the structure it does have is tailored to our individual needs. This room to be ourselves, without a lot of extraneous baggage, is the essence of simplicity, the topic we'll look at next.

chapter 4

Return to Simplicity

Letting go of complexity
I return to my nature—
pure and simple being.

It is so light and spacious!
There is room for every sensation.
Taking pleasure in simple movements
and simple things,
Life brings joy.

This is the essence of simplicity—to be light and spacious, free of unnecessary complexity. When we have learned to appreciate simplicity, we accept that each thing is enough just as it is, as we are enough just as we are in our simple, naked being.

SIMPLE PLEASURES

As we see in the verse above, the simple life has simple pleasures. There are several things that make this so. One is that when we eliminate the excess clutter, we have room inside to experience each moment more completely. Even small things are taken in deeply and can nourish us. The sound of the rain, an act of kindness, the relaxation of a sigh all become a source of pleasure.

More fundamental yet is the fact that our being is a source of pleasure. I am not referring so much to mind and body here (although these can certainly be a source of pleasure), but to our more essential nature, which is rich beyond imagination. It is full of depth and power and dynamism and peace and stillness and love and radiating light. Both full and empty, it is everything and no-thing. It is as endless as the night sky, and as full of stars. Most of the time, we are unaware of this underlying nature because we are caught in the contents of our mind. It is only when we can go beyond these contents that we come to know the vastness of our own being. This is the spiritual quest.

THE SIMPLICITY OF BEING

One of the meanings of the word *simple* is to be oneself without facade, to be free from artificiality and display. Unfortunately, few of us are free to live this way. We learned very early in life that there are ways we should act and ways we should not act. In conforming to what the world around us demanded, we lost touch with parts of ourselves. This feeds the development of a false self and keeps us busy trying to maintain it. The more we are cut off from the richness and substantiality of our true being, the harder we have to work to bolster our self-image so that we feel as if we are somebody.

In a recent presentation titled "Free to be Nobody," I said that until we are free to be nobody we are not really free to be ourselves. As long as we have an image to maintain, we can't be absolutely true to who we are. I invited the participants to examine the expectations that were still influencing them and then took the group through a guided meditation to go a little deeper. I asked them what it would feel like if they let go of all the effort it took to live up to the expectations they had taken on. The words that came back were peaceful, relaxed, open, free, joyful. These are qualities of being. True nature is peaceful, relaxed, open, free, and joyful. True nature is simple, because it is simply itself.

When something is simply itself, without anything else mixed in, it can be said to be pure. Purity is valued in spiritual work, particularly the purity of one's being. We must be careful not to get moralistic here however. Purification is not the righteous eradication of what is morally reprehensible. To be purified is simply to take away the impurities, the extra stuff laid on top of our underlying nature. When we take away the ego layer of image and activity, we come back to our essential nature in its more pristine condition. Coming back to this simplicity is what contemplative life is all about.

VOLUNTARY SIMPLICITY

It is not easy to be simple when we are totally absorbed in the complexities of modern life. We are barraged with choices, overwhelmed by the volume of stimuli we must deal with. If life came with an instruction manual for living in this complicated age, it would be volumes long.

Is it any surprise, then, that we are met in the bookstores with a number of best-selling books on how to simplify our lives? Simplifying has become one of the leading movements of the 90s. Elaine St. James, a top-selling author, reports that 30 percent of people are voluntarily downshifting in order to gain more time for themselves.[1] More would probably like to. Sixty-nine percent of Americans surveyed for a *Time* cover story in 1991 said they would like to slow down and find a more relaxed way to live.[2] We are at last discovering that having more and doing more is not necessarily the good life.

---

1. Elaine St. James, *Living the Simple Life* (New York: Hyperion, 1996), p.7.
2. Duane Elgin, *Voluntary Simplicity: Toward a Way of Life that Is Outwardly Simple, Inwardly Rich* (New York: William Morrow, 1993), p. 44.

These books give practical suggestions for how to cut out the unwanted clutter in our lives. They show us how to celebrate the quiet joys, simple pleasures, and everyday epiphanies of life, to borrow the phraseology of the author Sarah Ban Breathnach.[3]

These values are not new. Many of the world's great spiritual traditions have long advocated keeping the outer life simple so that one can give more attention to the inner life. But there are additional reasons now—big reasons, things we cannot overlook. "Unless dramatic changes are made in the manner of living and consuming in industrialized nations, we will soon produce a world of monumental destruction, suffering, conflict, and despair."[4] So writes analyst Duane Elgin in his book, *Voluntary Simplicity*. He outlines a number of possible futures and what needs to happen to build a revitalized, sustainable global culture.

Elgin's assessment of the ecological, economic, and social circumstances informs an urgent plea for change, yet he recognizes that the choice to live a life of voluntary simplicity comes from the heart. After listening to many who were living this lifestyle in the late 1970s, Elgin reported that a life of voluntary simplicity was not something people were persuaded to live, but rather something that came from deep soul-searching and evolved organically over a number of years. It grew out of a desire for a more balanced life and from a concern for the whole. Several people emphasized that it was not a matter of exterior changes as much as internal priorities.

---

3. Sarah Ban Breathnach, *Simple Abundance: A Daybook for Comfort and Joy* (New York: Warner, 1995).
4. Duana Elgin, *Voluntary Simplicity*, p. 53.

Elgin concluded (as had many before him) that there is no one recipe for a simple life and that part of what makes a life simple is that it is tailored to each individual's life purpose. This purpose becomes a filter that weeds out what, for that person, is merely a distraction, a frivolous use of their energy.

How important this is! When we get overwhelmed, one of the first things we lose is our ability to prioritize. We are at the mercy of a thousand different stimuli, all competing for our attention. Living "closer to the bone" in terms of what is important provides a focus and makes more time and energy available to invest in what really matters.

Penetrating deeply into the consciousness aspects of voluntary simplicity, Elgin suggests that to live *voluntarily*, we have to be present in the moment. When we are unconscious, we just continue the patterns of the past and are not living in a way that is free. Only when we are here, in the moment, are we in touch with the direct experience of who we are. This, in turn, leads us to discover our unity with what we call God, the Tao, and many other names.

HOLY AND UNHOLY POVERTY

Throughout human history, a large proportion of Earth's people have been poor. Most of the time, they've had no choice. Such poverty is usually disempowering. When we must put all of our energy into trying to physically survive, we seldom thrive.

The solution to this unholy poverty, according to Elgin, lies with those who live in relative abundance and can, through voluntary simplicity, share their resources with those who are less fortunate. This is what the religious traditions that have advocated simple living have always said. To give is the essence of charitable love.

A very small number of people have chosen poverty as part of a spiritual path. We might call this holy poverty, in that it serves the holy purposes of service to others and trust in God. This voluntary poverty is not just simple moderation, but a complete dispossession of all belongings. Perhaps the most joyful example of this was St. Francis of Assisi. Francis took poverty and made it an ideal—Lady Poverty—whom he could serve with great love and devotion. Describing St. Francis and his wandering monks, St. Bonaventura said, "Because they possessed nothing earthly, loved nothing earthly, and feared to lose nothing earthly, they were secure in all places."[5] The world was their monastery.

There is a certain freedom in this. When it no longer matters what clothes we wear or where we lay our heads to sleep, we are more available to the inner life. As Thomas Merton said, "As long as we remain poor, as long as we are empty and interested in nothing but God, we cannot be distracted."[6]

It is not easy to give up one's belongings and follow this path of voluntary poverty. Gandhi described it as a slow and painful process. Over a period of years, it became easier for him, and Gandhi eventually found joy in giving up his things. He said that although few of us could live up to the ideal of letting God provide for all of our needs, we should keep the ideal in view and critically examine our possessions with an eye to reducing them. His own vow of voluntary poverty was to possess nothing that he did not need.[7]

---

5. Goldian VandenBroeck, ed., *Less Is More: The Art of Voluntary Poverty* (Rochester, VT: Inner Traditions, 1978, 1996), pp. 37–38.
6. Thomas Merton, *Thoughts in Solitude* (Boston: Shambhala, 1993), p. 103.
7. Goldian VandenBroeck, ed., *Less Is More: The Art of Voluntary Poverty*, p. 60.

Of course, it takes more than just letting go of your possessions. If you give up all of your belongings and yet remain attached, you are not free. You are not what the Christian tradition has called "poor in spirit," because you have not let go of your possessiveness inside. It is this possessiveness that obstructs spiritual life. It is not material poverty, but rather nonattachment that is critical. It is possible to be "poor in spirit" and rich in the things of the world.

A Misunderstanding of Abundance

There is a lot of New Age talk about abundance and "prosperity consciousness" that I think creates more confusion, guilt, and more craving than is helpful at this time. This talk is based on the old, unquestioned assumption that there is a connection between how much you own and how valuable you are. A number of authors piggyback on this felt connection and package it in a particular way to suggest that any self-respecting person deserves a generous portion of the world's resources. "Prosperity consciousness" then becomes a matter of knowing that one deserves more. Although this is justified using a philosophy that sounds spiritual, I see nothing spiritual about it. It is the ego using what may be valid metaphysical principles to satisfy its own desires.

It concerns me to see the harm that comes out of this way of thinking. I know of a young family who has been falling further and further into debt over a number of years. They borrowed money so their home would not be foreclosed. Then, after going to a weekend pump-you-up training, they reversed their decision to scale back to a simpler lifestyle. Scaling back had become associated with staying small, and what they valued was a "big life." Do you see the confusion of levels here? A big life doesn't need to mean big spending and big debt. A big life can mean honestly facing the truth of one's circumstances. A big life can be one of voluntary poverty. Would anyone dare say Mother Teresa did not have a big life?

The problem comes from seeing material well-being as a sign of right alignment. This furthers the self-blame of the poor in the same way that the think-yourself-to-health philosophy contributes to the guilt of those who are sick. It takes what may be a valid component and makes it the whole picture. In this case, it says that if you are poor, you must be doing something wrong. After all, the nature of reality is abundance.

This argument misses an essential point. The natural abundance of reality is not individually owned, but is a characteristic of reality itself. To try to separate it from that reality is like skimming the reflection off the surface of the water. Yes, the nature of reality is abundance, but we participate in that abundance more fully when we do not remove ourselves from its stream.

It is being here, in the moment, that brings this richness to life, not barricading ourselves behind possessions. I'm not suggesting that possessions are bad. But when our possessions become a source of anxiety rather than enjoyment, when we can't bear to let them go, when we mistakenly believe that our possessions reflect our inner worth, then our possessions own us. We do not understand that our belongings mean nothing outside the practical value and enjoyment we get from them.

My beef with many of the prosperity teachings is that they forget this—at least, they allow us to forget it. They put so much emphasis on getting what we want that we begin to equate these external things with happiness. We forget that an abundant life is abundant in lessons, abundant in sorrow and joy, abundant in challenges. It may or may not be abundant in material possessions, and we need to be okay with that.

Just as the Taoist accepts rain and sunshine equally, the wise person accepts with equanimity what is presented. If there is financial comfort, we can enjoy it without clinging or making too much of it. We can recognize it as part of the natural flow, to be shared, so that the lives of others can also be more pleasant. If, on the other hand, there is little money, this is no reason to feel humiliated. We can still cultivate a sense of plenty. The attitude of the wise is thus a divine and joyful indifference.

We circle back, then, to the essence of simplicity, which is to be unencumbered, to be open and free, and to accept things as they are. Reducing the clutter in our outer lives helps, but the key is inner simplicity. When we are simple inside, we do not need to cast off all of our possessions or hide from the world. The Dalai Lama can travel from city to city, engaged in a busy life, without it jeopardizing an inner core of simplicity that radiates to everyone he meets.

chapter 5

The Middle Way

In the Tao's Middle Way
the only rule is this:
Abstain when there is reason to abstain,
enjoy what is there to enjoy,
never dividing sacred from mundane.
It is one gracious whole
giving you Itself.
Keep your eye on this.

What a simple rule: Abstain when there is reason to abstain, and enjoy what is there to enjoy. Sounds easy, but it's not. We seem to have a disposition to lean toward either enjoyment or self-restraint based on our character structure and to be weak in the other direction. It is even possible that both capacities are impaired, so that we can neither really enjoy ourselves nor control our impulses. Because these issues are so important, it is good to look at them in more detail.

The fact that most people have far too little restraint is readily apparent. How many people are in credit card debt because they couldn't say no? How many feel regret about sexual encounters or harsh words said in anger? How many suffer from being overweight because they can't pass up their favorite food? How many require constant stimulation and instant gratification? It seems obvious, if you look around, that we haven't learned the art of simple restraint.

I think there are many reasons for this. Although there is often a physiological underpinning to poor impulse control, the whole culture supports it. Our economy is based on stimulating desires and having them immediately gratified. There are also many psychological factors that contribute to the situation. I once had a friend who couldn't stand for me to have something that she didn't also have. It wasn't that she needed the same things I needed, but it seemed very painful for her to feel that she was being deprived of something. I think it reminded her of the intolerable pain of being without her mother's love.

I notice this same trait in many people. The orientation is toward having as little pain and as much enjoyment as possible. The gratification of desires functions like a salve, soothing a deep frustration. I talk about it later in the chapter as a way of filling psychological "holes." These are defensive, "negative" reasons why people move toward pleasure and away from pain, a phenomenon many see as inherent to the ego-self.

Given this tendency, it is interesting that some people are actually more comfortable when they are depriving themselves than when they are enjoying themselves. Surprising as this may seem, it is more widespread than you would think. There is a lot of psychological damage in this culture, and it shows up in both tendencies. When our self-esteem is wounded, we both try to patch it up through comforts and acquisitions and we act it out through self-sabotage and deprivation.

A client told me recently that she didn't enjoy the money she made early in her career as a businesswoman because she felt unworthy of it. This makes perfect sense, given her back-ground. As a child, she was passed from home to home, no one ever really valuing her. Later in life, this made it hard for her to treat herself as if she had value.

Sometimes when we have a history like this, it is adaptive to learn to "do without." Not wanting what isn't there can save a person a lot of grief and frustration. It can feel far safer to limit our desires than to be left open and vulnerable, wanting something.

This pattern of self-deprivation can show up in many ways. We see it played out on the emotional level when we don't really take in the love and attention that others are willing to give. We see it in the material realm when we can't earn, or keep, or spend money. It shows up when we sabotage our dreams or fail to live up to our capacities, when we deprive ourselves of little pleasures that come with self-love, and when we ignore the needs of our bodies. It shows up when we don't embrace ourselves.

Since much of our enjoyment is related to the capacity to fully inhabit our bodies, it is worth taking some time to understand what makes this difficult. Certainly many of our forebears had a deep mistrust of the pleasures of the body. Often this mistrust has religious roots, but it is passed through the generations in a more personal way. For example, a woman who is not comfortable with her body will communicate that discomfort to her child, and that child will grow up feeling it is not okay to exist and take pleasure in the physical realm. She will grow up alienated from her own sensual nature.

This deep rejection of the body feeds many of the social problems we face today. Much violence stems from a lack of appropriate touch and from not being able to integrate our sexuality in a healthy way. We get addicted to "big sensation" because we are so conflicted that we cannot feel ordinary sensation. We've lost our connection to the true pleasure and sensuality of our being.

When I referred to religious influences, I was not only talking about puritanical values, but also their deeper foundation. Long before we split the atom, we split spirit from matter, conceptualizing them as separate realms. This division, with its consequent denigration of the physical world, is largely responsible for our mistrust of the senses and our mistreatment of the environment. If we saw Earth as sacred, we could not abuse it in the way we do.

The resurgence of interest in Earth-based and goddess religions, as well as in creation-centered spirituality, is helping to restore the balance. When we bring spirit and matter back together again, it helps us become whole. We can heal the planet and heal ourselves. Spiritual life takes on new meaning when we realize that we can see, hear, taste, smell, and feel God too.

Perhaps the biggest reason we find it hard to stay present in our bodies is that we're running away from our inner experience, particularly our emotions. If we stay present in the body, we'll need to feel all of our conflicts, our undigested pain, our animal instincts. We'll become more human.

THE CAPACITY FOR RESTRAINT

To be a truly sensitive human being, living a sane and balanced life and enjoying the pleasures of that, we need not only the capacity for enjoyment, but also the capacity for restraint. This is not a matter of morality as much as practicality. Gluttony dulls our capacity to experience pleasure. When we are busy grabbing for more, we can't enjoy what we have. We lose the pleasure of getting up from a satisfying meal, feeling just right.

Exploration: *Gluttony*

Take a few minutes to look at your life. Where in your life is it hard to say no? Which desires seem to control you? When you don't say no, how do you feel? Imagine yourself in a tempting situation, foregoing the pleasure of the moment. How might that feel?

One definition of indulgence is knowing that something is not in your best interest, but doing it anyway. You may justify giving in to desire by arguing that you deserve it, that you are pampering yourself because you love yourself, but this is not true or objective love. Indulgence comes with a price. It actually perpetuates self-hate. Viewed from this perspective, restraint is not the denial of pleasure but rather the protector of it.

In addition to taking responsibility for our own well-being, we may also forego pleasures for the sake of something outside of us. We may, for example, go on a fast in support of a cause. We may forego an adulterous affair out of respect for our mate. We may abstain from buying something because our purchase would be based on economic exploitation or is not good for Earth.

Some find it useful to have guidelines to follow. Thich Nhat Hanh has written a new version of the Buddhist precepts called Five Wonderful Precepts[1] In each of the five precepts, there is a commitment to develop positive behaviors and to practice some form of restraint. Positive behaviors include the commitment to develop loving speech, to practice mindful eating, drinking, and consuming, to practice generosity, and to cultivate compassion. The restraints include vows to not gossip, to not possess what should belong to others, to not condone killing, to refrain from sexual relations that may hurt others, and to not ingest books, films, TV programs, or conversations that can have a toxic effect. Following precepts such as these can help refine our consciousness and restore our innate sensitivities, as well as our sense of discipline, so that we can perhaps later follow our own guidance.

---

1. Thich Nhat Hanh, *For a Future to Be Possible* (Berkeley: Parallax Press, 1993).

There are many things that cause us to lose our innate sensitivity and sense of balance. Probably the primary one is doing things to escape or avoid uncomfortable feelings. When we do this repetitively and compulsively, we have an addiction. We now recognize not only substance addictions, but also process addictions. These are our addictions to activities and states. Examples include addictions to work, exercise, sex, shopping, and love relationships. We get so caught in the addiction, that we lose sight of what it's doing to us. The following exercise can help restore awareness.

Exploration: *Practicing Restraint*

Think of one harmful habit you have and create an aim to refrain from it for a certain amount of time. (I suggest you start with something like two weeks.) During this time, your job is not only to practice restraint, but also to notice what makes it difficult. You want to find out as much as you can about what fuels this habit and what purpose it serves. The habit of binge eating, for example, may serve the purpose of keeping down certain feelings. By refraining (or trying to refrain), you can learn more about the dynamics involved.

It is obvious that our "no" needs to be quite firm at times. Breaking addictive patterns is not easy. Yet there are other times when the "no" can be softer, because it is part of a natural ebb and flow. For example, an animal will often stop eating when it is sick. With a return to health, it will resume feeding.

Our rigid beliefs interfere with this natural intelligence. We can be so far out of touch with our actual needs that we endanger our lives by doing what we believe is right. Other times, it's our unconscious motives that muddy the picture. We use abstinence, for example, to cover up areas of conflict. This is perhaps most easily seen in the area of sexuality. It can be easier to play holy and to "transcend" than it is to deal with the vulnerability involved in sexual intimacy. This same avoidance can come into play in creating a solitary life or eschewing the material world. We may think we are doing it for spiritual reasons when, really, defensive motivations are running the show.

In the Tao's middle way, we use restraint with clarity and wisdom. We're not just following rules because someone says so. We're not using restraint to hide, and we're not doing it to punish ourselves. We use restraint to create balance in a life that is not too tight and not too loose.

RENUNCIATION WITHOUT PAIN

We can see from the above discussion that we can decide to limit or abstain from something without making it "bad." It is much better when we can let go of things without needing to reject them. Rejection involves a charge; there is unfinished business. The more attachment there is to something, the more force we have to use to push it away. We have to push ourselves away because we don't really want to let go.

It doesn't have to be like this. We can let go because we see the wisdom of letting go. Renunciation can be part of a natural unfoldment in which we let go of what we no longer need. This should sound familiar after our last chapter. At this level, renunciation is like voluntary simplicity. Sufi master Hazrat Inayat Khan points out the practical side of this.

One need not learn renunciation; life itself teaches it; and to the small extent that one has to learn a lesson in the path of renuncia-tion, it is this: that in the case where in order to gain silver coins one has to lose the copper ones, one must learn to lose them. That is

the only unselfishness one must learn: that one cannot have both
the copper and the silver.[2]

We give up the copper to get the silver, and we give up the silver to get the gold. This mirrors our development. We give up crawling in order to walk. On the spiritual journey, we give up the pleasures of the small self for the much greater pleasure of freedom.

He continues, "The wise therefore renounce willingly what they feel like renouncing; but they are constantly in pursuit of what they feel like gaining."[3] Learning to say "yes" is just as important as learning to say "no."

Whether we say yes or no depends on the needs of the moment. Renunciation is being able to take it or leave it, according to what is necessary. In this sense, renunciation is not so much a discipline as a discrimination, a clear seeing of the situation. It is the nonattachment that allows us to do what is best.

It has been said that, once we renounce the desire, we do not need to renounce its object. In other words, it is the attachment we must relinquish. When we're not attached, enjoying the object of desire creates no problem. This, I believe, is fairly well known and is central to our discussion. The problem comes not with enjoying something; the problem comes with trying to hold on to it.

The wisdom of insecurity lies in recognizing that we can't really hold on to anything. In Buddhist terms, it is understanding impermanence. It is understanding that nothing lasts and that it is the effort to hold on that causes suffering. I know of a

---

2. Hazrat Inayat Khan, *The Art of Personality*, The Sufi Message, vol. VIII (Delhi: Motilal Banarsidass, 1989/1994), p. 260.
3. Hazrat Inayat Khan, *The Art of Personality*, p. 259.

rather wealthy woman whose money has become a burden. She feels compelled to protect it at all costs, yet is no longer able to enjoy it. She is like a cramped hand that cannot let go. When we remember that we don't truly own anything, and that whatever we have is "on loan" from the universe, we can enjoy much more. We can enjoy both the things on loan to us and also those on loan to other people. I can walk down a street with beautifully landscaped gardens and enjoy them every bit as much as do the people living in the big houses next to them. When we see that our lives themselves are on loan (and that perhaps that loan is about to be foreclosed), this can bring a deep appreciation for each passing moment.

THE GIFTS OF DETACHMENT

It is easy to confuse detachment with a cold, unfeeling attitude that is really the ego's attempt at detachment. Real detachment is not an emotional cut-off; it is not a refusal to feel. Detachment allows us to access a full range of experiences without clinging to any of them. Detachment is the lack of strings, the lack of attachment. It leaves us very open.

One of the gifts of detachment is that it allows us to enjoy more of our experience. When there is no pulling or pushing, how can we not enjoy? Some would say that this is the only time we can really enjoy because we are not busy trying to advance our own agendas.

Another gift of detachment is that it allows us to engage more fully and more freely. We've all had the experience of being in a situation (a job interview, a presentation, a date) where we were strongly invested in a particular outcome. It puts the pressure on, and we're uptight. Enjoyment, on the other hand, comes with relaxation. It comes with spontaneity and the freedom to be oneself.

Detachment also creates more room for the truth to emerge. If we are clinging to a particular outcome, we are not so able to see the bigger picture. We miss the grace that is working behind the scenes. I have found that what the universe has in store for me is often better than my fixation on the outcome. Stepping away from my attachment helps me remember this. Detachment is thus the inner attitude that allows us to refrain when there is reason to refrain, and enjoy what is there to enjoy.

THE CAPACITY FOR ENJOYMENT

To not enjoy life is to slap God in the face. It is to be given a gift and not say "thank you." Enjoyment is part of the thank you. It is a natural response to seeing the beauty of something.

I want to share an experience that has helped me realize this. It is not an uncommon experience; you may have had it, too. It is the sense of being overwhelmed by the magnificence and beauty of nature. How deeply I am touched seems to be a function of how open my heart is. The more open I am, the more I am dazzled by the beauty. I recognize that the splendor is always present, but that most of the time, I am "dulling it down," filtering it through a mind that is preoccupied. This is why stillness is the birther of fresh perception. When I am still, I am not looking through that filter, and I can perceive things in their naked beauty.

To have that openness, we have to loosen the internal structures that bind us. Many of these relate to the expectations that were set for us as children and from the conclusions we drew, based on insufficient information. For example, I have noticed that many people harbor a deep-seated belief that who they are is "too much." When asked what is "too much," they may answer that their emotions are "too much," their intensity is "too much," their aliveness or their needs are "too much." The "too much" is a judgment that comes in response to the reactions of others. Very often, certain qualities in a child are uncomfortable for a parent, and the parent responds in a less than supportive way. Not understanding that it's really the parent's limitation, the child falsely concludes that whatever she or he was in touch with at the time must have been "too much." The long-term consequences of this belief can be devastating. It leads, not only to a loss of self-esteem, but also to a constant holding back.

I think we are all doing this in our own ways. Like a governor on a car limiting its speed, we have governors on our exuberance, our pleasure, our expansion, our enjoyment. This isn't hard to feel. Just try stepping over the line. I recently found myself enjoying my life so much that I felt a little naughty! This is good, I thought. If I live in such a way that I feel a little naughty (in the way a child might feel naughty for not following the rules), I will be pushing beyond the conditioning and control of my inner governor.

Rather than thinking of enjoyment as an obstacle to spiritual "progress," we should think of it as a path. True enjoyment comes when we see the goodness in life, the absolute opulence of spirit informing every aspect of our experience. Enjoyment is loving the Tao in both its nameless aspect and its countless faces.

The Tao's Middle Way

We can learn to discriminate between those times when fulfilling our desires hurts us and when it is exactly what we need. There are desires whose fulfillment distracts us and desires whose fulfillment makes us more whole. We can't divide them by their content, only by their role in our lives.

The desires we want to be most careful about are those that are used to "fill our holes."[4] A hole is a place where we have become numb to some part of our essence and consequently feel that something is missing in us; we are deficient in some way. Because these holes are so painful to feel, we try to avoid feeling them by "filling them" with goodies from the world. We gather accomplishments, for example, to make up for our sense of inadequacy, or we chase after admiration to cover over our shame. In a sense, everything we do that is fueled by the need to bolster our sense of self is motivated by a hole. According to this theory, the need for recognition, love, status, power, and so forth are not really inherent needs, but are the result of losing parts of ourselves. Filling these holes with goodies from the outside may be comforting to the ego, but the solution is only temporary. Since what is missing is a part of our own essential nature, it is far better to stay with the painful feelings and retrieve what was lost than to compensate with a second-rate substitute.

There are other needs that are not so much the result of being cut off from essence as they are from being aligned with essence. The late humanist psychologist Abraham Maslow might have called them *metaneeds*. They are needs to fulfill our capacities and to be all of ourselves. They motivate our self-actualization and our Self-Realization. We must embrace these needs if we are to follow our hearts and realize our destinies.

And then there are the desires that are not necessarily so grand, but are simply a part of everyday life. A friend of mine recently challenged the idea that desires are bottomless and that we should therefore learn to transcend them. In support of this,

---

4. The concept of holes has been developed by A. H. Almaas, particularly in his book, *Diamond Heart, Book One* (Berkeley: Diamond Books, 1987).

she told me that throughout her childhood, she had wanted to have a dog. When she finally got one as an adult, she found this very fulfilling. It wasn't a bottomless need at all. It was met very specifically by having one dog. My friend felt the same way about many other "human needs." The need for touch, for example, isn't bottomless. Getting the touch we need leaves us more open, and this is a good thing.

I find it helpful to remember that our human needs are part of the sacredness. Only when I embrace all of me, can I gravitate to a way of living that is in harmony with my flow.

chapter 6

Sometimes Two, Sometimes One

Two paths return home.
One, the path of solitude
where I am alone with God.
The other, the path of relationship
where my human beloved
strips me naked
making me ready for Love.

Two paths, intersecting.
Sometimes there are two of us
sometimes only one.

Traditionally, the path of the contemplative has been one of
solitude. Some, like Trappist monk Thomas Merton, consider
the only true contemplatives to be those who live the monastic
life. Certainly, there is a long heritage of seekers who have left
the world in order to devote themselves to God in this way.
There is also a heritage of religious people who have gone into
the world and sought out the most needy in order to serve God.
And there are some who use love relationships as a path of
awakening. Holding to my earlier depiction of contemplation as
the yin side of spiritual life, I think all of these qualify. We can
be receptive to God when we are alone, in community, and in
the arms of our human beloved.

THE PATH OF SOLITUDE

Solitude is not the same as isolation. Isolation is driven by the need for protection, which means it is a kind of defense. It doesn't matter whether the isolation is physical or psychological; it is a form of being unavailable, hiding behind a barrier.

Solitude, in contrast, is open and at ease. It is a choice made in the moment, not a character position. Solitude is part of a natural cycle, easily entered into and easily dropped. It is like the natural balance of inbreath and outbreath. We wander away from the crowd to be alone for a while, coming back when we are ready.

Thus solitude is not a turning away from contact so much as a rest from contact, a time to come back to ourselves. There can be a great deal of intimacy in this. We can support it by creating an intimate setting within our environment, but mostly it comes from being in contact with ourselves emotionally and spiritually. Intimacy comes with being personal, and solitude gives us an opportunity for this.

When we are alone with ourselves, we have the opportunity to face many things, some of them painful. Some people avoid solitude for this reason. We can also be affected by judgments we have about what it means to be alone. The exercise on p. 49 can be used to flush out what some of these judgments and concerns are.

Of course, much of the time when we are physically alone, we are still carrying our relationships around inside of us. There may be a conflict or a decision we need to think about, but part of it is that we simply like the company. We like the connection. We don't really want to feel alone.

Some say that we are almost never alone inside because our ego structure is itself made of internalized relationships. This

---

Exploration: *What It Means to Be Alone*

You will need a piece of paper for this exercise. At the top of the page write, "Being alone . . . ." You will use this as a prompt for your own responses. Each time you read the opening words, write down how you would complete the sentence. Then read it again, and let a new response come. You want to find out as much as you can, so I suggest completing the sentence until you have really run dry. An exercise like this can start the ball rolling. It's worth following up by free writing about the responses that stand out to you, or talking about them with a friend.

---

means that my sense of self comes from all those interactions in the past that are still present as part of me. These internalized relationships involve memories of how we felt with another and of our images of both self and other. When all the feelings are metabolized and we recognize that the images are no longer accurate, these internalized relationships can dissolve; we begin to feel alone in a new and fresh way. It is perhaps the first time that we are really alone.

Thomas Merton once wrote, "As soon as you are really alone, you are with God."[1] I think he was saying that we have to drop our other concerns to feel God's presence, and that God is always here. We can explain it within the framework I was just using by saying that, when we are really alone inside, our ego structure is not active and disappears for the moment. What is left is the larger reality of Being, which in many traditions is called God.

---

1. Thomas Merton, *Thoughts in Solitude* (Boston, Shambhala, 1933), p.130.

THE PATH OF CONSCIOUS RELATIONSHIP

In his books, *Journey of the Heart* and *Love and Awakening*, psychologist John Welwood suggests that intimate love relationships can help us face ourselves more rapidly than any other aspect of worldly life.[2] Many others have said the same. Relationships can show us aspects of ourselves from which we have been hiding and can open up places that have been closed.

We are often drawn to our partners precisely because they are living out aspects of ourselves that we have not yet consciously integrated. If we are to use the relationship as a vehicle for growth, we will not be content to let this person be "our other half," but will challenge ourselves to develop those parts that the partner is filling in for. For example, if I am drawn to my partner's freedom and spontaneity, I will want to recover my own freedom and spontaneity, not just enjoy it in my partner.

We can use not only what attracts us but also what repels us as a mirror. What we react to in our partners in a negative way usually reflects parts of ourselves that we have rejected and closed down. I may, for example, react negatively to my partner's needs for attention because I do not accept and understand my own denied needs for attention. Rather than making my partner wrong, I can use the reaction to find out more about what is incomplete in myself.

Another way that love relationships can serve our spiritual development is by taking us beyond self-absorption. It is not often we let go of ourselves as the center of the universe, and

---

2. John Welwood, *Journey of the Heart: Intimate Relationship and the Path of Love* (New York: Harper Perennial, 1990); and *Love and Awakening: Discovering the Sacred Path of Intimate Relationship* (New York: HarperCollins, 1996).

yet it is absolutely necessary in order to expand beyond the confines of the ego-self. When we love, we are so absorbed by our experience of the other that we let go of this self for a while. We get larger.

As love beckons us to expand, whatever is in the way of that expansion comes up as an issue or barrier. For example, after opening up to someone and growing really close, we often feel scared and find ways to back off. We might find fault with the other person as an excuse to withdraw, or as a way to move away from our feelings of love and vulnerability. If we are on a path of becoming more conscious, we will notice this fault-finding and try not to take it too seriously. We will look beyond our immediate reaction and discover what motivates it. Perhaps there is a fear that being vulnerable will inevitably lead to being hurt. That awareness, in turn, may prompt us to remember how we were hurt in an earlier relationship, and we may then metabolize and release those feelings.

Real intimacy, sooner or later, exposes all of our contractions. We come to one turning point after another in which we can either face our pain and fear, or retreat from love. There are times when the pain is so great that we can't do anything but retreat, yet love is a worthy opponent. Love grabs hold of us and does not let us go. It keeps our feet to the fire, forcing us again and again to grapple with our limitations and vulnerabilities. Part of what makes love such a worthy opponent is that it is so sweet. Love melts us, opening us to everything around us and inside of us. With this kind of impact, how can relationship not be a path of awakening? How can it not be a path to God?

THE URGE TO MERGE

I think the deepest desire played out in our love relationships is the urge to merge. You want to become so close that there is nothing separating you from your beloved, so close that you are one.

What we are really striving for, according to spiritual teacher Hameed Ali, is to feel that part of our own essence that melts the boundaries and releases us from separation.[3] We associate that merging quality with a love relationship, although it can be felt in other situations as well. We may feel ourselves merged with nature, merged with everyone we come in contact with, merged with our own True Self. It is the drive toward unity that inspires much of the world's mystical poetry and drives the spiritual search.

What, then, if we look at our attempts to create a merged relationship, not from the psychological perspective (where the answer to fusion and codependency is to fortify personal boundaries and create a stronger sense of individuality), but from a spiritual perspective in which the urge to merge with another person is a misplaced longing for the oneness of unity consciousness?

Ironically, what we are ultimately seeking, if Ali is right, eludes us when we become attached to another person. This is clear when you understand what unity consciousness is and what attachment is. In unity consciousness, there is no "I." It is the default value when we stop perceiving from the viewpoint of the separate self. In that moment, we know ourselves as the oneness in everything. Attachment, on the other hand, is an attempt to eliminate separation, but it is based on separation. It comes when we identify with the separate self. I, in this body, feel attached to you, in another. If we can let go of this identifi-

---

3. This is called "Merging Essence" by Ali in his teaching known as the Diamond Approach. This perspective has been described most fully in his teachings on Merging Love, not yet in published form.

cation and feel our more boundless essential nature, we are no longer a point trying to hold onto another point, but two fields interpenetrating. There is a oneness possible here that is not possible on the physical plane. When we realize the nonlocal nature of essence, we realize what cannot be lost. Holding on doesn't make sense in the same way. Only in true openness can real union be found.

SOMETIMES TWO, SOMETIMES ONE

I remember once watching two birds soar overhead. I was reflecting on the place of relationships in my life and I noticed what an easy interplay there was between these birds. Sometimes they flew together, and sometimes they flew alone. These two movements flowed into one another, back and forth. Sometimes two, sometimes one.

Each of us has our own rhythm of solitude and togetherness. How wonderful it is to plumb the depths of ourselves in both conditions and use each to strengthen the other. Both are achievements. Certainly, it is no easy thing to make ourselves vulnerable to love. It is also not easy to be alone. It took me a long time to go from isolation and loneliness to the gifts of true solitude. I had to work through a lot of painful feelings and learn that I could be a source of compassion and holding for myself. When I could do that, being alone no longer felt empty but full. The emptiness inside became like a clear sky through which the eagles fly.

Imagine for a moment two birds soaring. One finds an updraft and they take it together, spiraling heavenward. Love is an updraft; it is the strongest updraft I know. We don't need to do it alone. Whether it is community, a teacher, or a human lover, there are others we can travel with, assisting one another, propelled by the force of love itself.

In either case, whether we are alone or with others, there are moments when our boundaries dissolve and we find ourselves one with something larger. In the mystical life, sometimes there are two of us, and sometimes only one.

chapter 7

Dropping into Silence

Silence falls softly
like snow through the night
stilling all activity,
bringing a purity beyond belief,
the mind finding no purchase
in this passage to eternity.

Silence is the contemplative's way home. It is the stillness beneath the mind, the depth below the surface, the passage to eternity. It is a passage to eternity because it is outside of time. When there is nothing to track and no one tracking, time disappears, leaving only an eternal now.

Many who have gone very deeply into meditative states describe a gap in consciousness where everything disappears. This is perhaps the deepest dimension of silence. Silence, as we more often know it, refers to no reaction, no commentary, no grasping or rejection. The emotions are still, thoughts are few. No questions, no answers, just being.

STEPPING OUT OF MIND-SPIN

I am quite fond of a term I first heard from author and meditation teacher Stephen Levine. The term is *mind-spin*. It's a good word. To me, it captures both the activity of the mind, spinning like a top, and the product of that activity, a subjective reality we become caught in. When we examine our experience carefully, we see how quickly our perceptions of the outer world are replaced by a swirl of associations and embellishments. I look at a flower, for example, and the next thing I know I am remembering a flower someone gave me and what happened in that relationship, and there I am strolling down memory lane. Or I have an unpleasant interaction and soon I am lost in an undercurrent of old feelings where nothing ever seems to get better. The mind immediately abandons the stimulus in preference for its own creations.

As you can see from the last example, we go beyond the bare facts and spin yarns, tales about what is happening. Some of these tales are our favorite story lines and we spin new variations of them repeatedly, casting ourselves in the same roles over and over. It is not until we have learned to free our awareness that we can step back and "catch ourselves in the act." Only then can the story end.

Our mind-spin is very captivating. It is not just thinking—certainly not practical thinking about what we are doing—but a whole tapestry of thoughts, feelings, self-images, memories, and so on. To come back to reality, we must step out of this subjective world and come into the present moment.

There are many ways to step out of the mind-spin. We can come back to our immediate sensory experience; we can get absorbed in nonverbal tasks that quiet the mind; we can chant and meditate; we can whirl like the dervishes; or we can walk peacefully through our lives, letting silence fall softly like snow through the night.

It helps quiet the mind when we can abide in something deeper than our changing thoughts. Just as a large lake almost always has ripples across its surface, so thoughts continuously ripple through our consciousness. Certainly it helps for the surface part of the mind to be still, yet if we can identify with the deeper stillness, the silence can grow so strong that the ripples don't disturb it. This is a basic principle of many kinds of meditation. It is not so much that we stop our thoughts as that we learn how to be less caught in them.

MEDITATION AND CONTEMPLATIVE PRAYER

One of the oldest and most respected paths for entering silence is meditation. There are a number of different kinds of meditation being taught today. These generally fall into two camps: those that rely on concentration and those that center around mindfulness. Those that focus on concentration still the mind by focusing on one object, perhaps a mantra, a visualization, the breath, or a particular energy center. In this way, the mind is kept focused, one-pointed. We are so used to letting our minds run amok that this disciplining of mind has a profound quieting effect.

In mindfulness practices, we observe the workings of the mind. This is a shift that requires and reinforces distance from the contents of the mind. Rather than being lost in thoughts, we watch thoughts. This breaks the trance nature of our usual involvement.

Another name for this second type of meditation is awareness meditation. We are watching not only the patterns of our minds, but becoming aware of everything that is present. We open to our emotions, sensations, impulses, and subtle energies and learn to meet them in a way that is accepting rather than rejecting, compassionate rather than judgmental. Our goal is to become more present to each moment.

Often, concentration practices are combined with mindfulness. They help quiet the racing mind so that we can settle into the deeper nature of consciousness. Over time, our meditation practice will likely change in duration and in form. Often there is a progression from more structure to less.

For many years, I thought of meditation as a practice that revolved around discipline and control. I found it unnatural to try to exert mental control over my experience, and I resisted it. It took me a long time to understand that, at a deeper level, meditation is simply being with *what is* rather than trying to manipulate or change *what is*. It is letting the contents of the mind pass through without holding on to them or to the self we've taken ourselves to be. Not identifying with or contracting around the contents allows our awareness to expand, and we feel more of our essential nature. A friend told me that, for her, meditation is surrendering into presence. It is letting herself dissolve into pure being.

While meditation has been a staple of Eastern spirituality for thousands of years, methods for entering silence have often been neglected in the Christian tradition. In response to this need, Father Thomas Keating developed what he calls "Centering Prayer."[1] It is not so much a new form of prayer as an updated form of earlier teachings. The essence of the practice is to quiet oneself and become available to God. It is based not on concentrating, but on being receptive, soft, open. It involves sitting quietly for periods of at least twenty minutes twice a day and using a sacred word to gently refocus attention away from thoughts, feelings, and sensations back to the intention to open oneself to God.

The practice of Centering Prayer is intended as a preparation for a deeper stage of prayer called contemplative prayer. Contemplative prayer comes on its own and is considered a gift from spirit. It comes as years of rigorous discipline and traditional forms of prayer slowly give way to a prayer that is no

---

1. Father Thomas Keating, *Open Mind, Open Heart: The Contemplative Dimension of the Gospel* (New York: Continuum, 1995).

longer a discipline and no longer has words. Even the sense of someone praying disappears, until there is just a silent absorption into the presence of God.

SILENCE IN NATURE AND IN OUR LIVES

Nature has a quieting effect on me. Sometimes it takes a while to drop the concerns I have been carrying, but if I am open and can direct my attention to the physical details around me, I slowly slip into a natural state of silence. I say "a natural state of silence" because silence is a natural state. It is not our habitual condition, but one we feel at home in. You can see it in peoples' faces. It is easy to spot those who are actually here, in the moment, and those who are caught in a whirl of mental activity much like the cartoon character Pigpen, surrounded by a cloud of dirt.

It works both ways: consciously entering into nature with a quiet mind allows us to experience the natural world in a much more vivid and alive way, and paying attention to the sensory details of the natural world helps draw our attention away from the quicksand of the mind. Redirecting our attention back to sensation can therefore be used as a method, as it is sometimes used in sitting meditation.

Exploration: *Sensing in Nature*

Take a walk somewhere pleasant, holding the intention to really sink into sensory contact with the world around you. Each time you find yourself thinking, come back to what you see, hear, smell, and feel. Let this process of sensing totally captivate your attention with no need to evaluate or manage it. Enjoy the nuances of light and color, the feeling of the air against your skin, the sounds and smells of nature. When thoughts come, gently release them. Feel an openness in your heart as you walk.

Sometimes these shorter practices aren't enough and it takes a more extended period to drop into silence. If you feel wearied by the demands of life, the following experiment may prove a valuable method for clearing the space.

Exploration: *Drenched in Silence*

Take a couple of days and go somewhere by yourself. Places near water are especially good, although the desert and woods are also powerful places to encounter silence. The point is to put yourself at some distance from the busy world of commerce and entertainment and allow yourself to be emptied of all activity. Nothing to do, nothing to think about, nothing to find.

Some people will want to minimize physical activity so that they can feel totally relaxed. Others find it useful to get into their bodies again by taking long walks or engaging in other physical exercise. You need to find the balance that is right for you. It is fine to do a little journaling, especially if it is a way of staying close to yourself in the moment. Remember, however, the goal of writing is not to excavate your psyche or find new directions for your life. It is simply to help you be present. You are there to be drenched in silence.

I have written the above exercise as a solo venture in nature, but there are also retreat centers which are set up to simplify your daily needs by providing beds, meals, and other amenities. You might find it nourishing to be with others who are also taking time to step away from their daily lives and go inward.

Another option is to do a meditation retreat. Here, there is a structure and method to help you go into silence. Many find that a concentrated dose of meditation helps support their daily practice. If meditation is fairly new to you, you might want to select a retreat that allows the flexibility to attend or not attend specific sessions of sitting meditation. This way you don't need to fight against your own flow or resist an imposed structure. If, on the other hand, you like a tight structure and want to "trap" yourself into a discipline you would otherwise slip away from, there are meditation retreats that provide this. In either case, I suggest investigating the situation before putting yourself into it.

I have recently returned from a five-day silent meditation retreat of the flexible kind, and that suited me well. I could take care of my body so I wasn't constantly dealing with pain, and I could practice any way I like. I chose to go to the retreat because I was craving silence and was really ready to let go into it. This made the practice easy. I found myself letting go of method and just giving myself over, finding that balance I speak of in the next chapter between just sitting without goal or effort and the sense of opening to a beloved. Often I focused on the spaciousness in my heart. I watched myself become empty and then fill up again. I returned, not to the chatter of unfinished business, but to new creativity and the next unfoldment of my life.

While it is useful to set aside a period of days every so often to leave behind the demands of our daily lives, what we really need is to learn to live from greater silence. We need to bring the silence with us into the world. I'm not suggesting we go around refusing to speak, but that we cultivate that state of consciousness described at the beginning of the chapter. We learn to live with less commentary, less emotional reactivity, a quieter mind. Then when we speak, our words will come from a deeper place and will be heard differently. We won't be babbling on to others, giving voice to the random activity on the surface of our minds, but rather sharing our deeper wisdom. We also won't be babbling to ourselves so much, and thus will be able to enjoy the mysteries and pure being of the magical world we live in.

SILENCE AS GIFT

I can't think of anything as restful as complete silence. It is as if the great wheel of ego activity finally grinds to a halt and we drop into another dimension. It is pristine there, sparkling in its purity, a place of shining awareness that is absolutely still and clear.

In this chapter's opening verse, I said that silence descends as softly as the falling snow. It comes as a gift, not something we control. As meditation teacher Toni Packer has noted, emptiness and silence are not a place to be reached by methods.[2] They come with the end of striving, not as the result of it. I think this is true whether we are talking about the simple silence of a quiet mind or the silent communion of contemplative prayer. We can do the things that serve as preparation, but we can't force silence. We can only detach from the noise.

At first, our silence is fragile, too delicate to withstand much activity. It is like a hothouse flower requiring special conditions. As it becomes more deeply rooted, we are able to go about our lives without disturbing the deeper quiet. Thus, our silence grows.

---

2. Toni Packer, *The Work of This Moment* (Boston: Shambhala, 1990), p. 20.

chapter 8
Perfect Receptivity

To wait in silence
with empty hands
open and receptive,
the perfect yielding—
action without actor,
the emptiness so pristine
no footprints can be found.

This verse describes the contemplative posture. It is open and receptive, waiting with empty hands to accept what is given. To understand this more fully, we need to examine both what it means to "wait in silence," and what it means to have "empty hands." These will be explored in the next two sections.

TO WAIT IN SILENCE

What does it mean to wait in silence? In chapter 7, I described silence as a state of inner quiet. To wait in silence means to let the mind be still.

It is the concept of waiting that needs further development. When experienced meditators describe *just sitting*, they are not expecting something particular to happen and not trying to make anything happen. This is important. Over and over again, spiritual teachings tell us that the movement (external or internal) of going after something blocks our deeper realization. There are several reasons for this. First, it constricts our openness. It is as if grasping (and rejecting and all the other reactions of the little self) closes the aperture of our being. It is a contraction, a knot. Only in total openness do we fall into the larger reality. The attitude of grasping also reveals an identification with the ego, which will always feel separate and incomplete. This identification prevents us from knowing ourselves in our deeper nature, a nature that was never born and can never die. This may sound abstract to you, but it is the key to Self-Realization. We cannot realize who we are on the deepest level if we are identified with a more surface level. It is the surface level that goes after what the Taoists called "the myriad ten thousand things." Perhaps the simplest way to think about it is that if we are wanting things to be other than the way they are, we are not in harmony with the Tao and cannot be at peace.

Stopping the movement of aversion and desire is not easy. This movement goes on so automatically that we often do not notice it. The first step to changing a habit is to recognize it clearly. You might try the practice of noting each time you catch yourself moving toward something. Just say, *reaching, reaching*. This includes impulses toward physical objects and pleasures, but also toward intangibles like recognition, attention, and love. This habit is very deep and is not easily uprooted. Dropping the attitude of reaching is part of the open stance of contemplation.

We must learn to wait in a way that is not grasping. I think the best metaphor is to wait, like a lover, in softness and receptivity. Rather than chasing after the beloved, we wait for the beloved to come to us.

I propose that we put the two together: *not reaching* and *opening through love*. When we are not reaching, we are looser and more relaxed. We are not trying to control or acquire, and this may help dissolve our identification with ego. The other element, opening through love, is the essence of the feminine aspect. Love makes us soft and ready to be filled.

EMPTY HANDS

We should not miss the point that, in contemplation, we wait with empty hands. We wait, not with an attitude of entitlement, but as a beggar, appreciating what is given. This is repugnant to the ego. Ego does not want to be a beggar; it wants to be a prince. It is helpful, therefore, to explore what gets in the way of being nobody special.

Exploration: *Waiting with Empty Hands*

Lie on a comfortable surface, on your back with arms to the sides, palms up. Breathe through your heart and re-peat the phrase, *"I have nothing to give that you don't already have."* Do this for at least five minutes—longer, if you can stay with it. Let the feelings come. When you are ready, get up and write about the experience. What is it like to wait with empty hands? What feelings make it difficult?

Having nothing to give may expose feelings of being inadequate or undeserving. When we are bearing gifts, we feel as if we *are* something because we *have* something. We don't realize that the real gift is spiritual poverty: the knowledge that, without Being, we are just an empty shell. We must understand this completely before we are willing to drop the endless activity involved in trying to be somebody. As we mature in spiritual work, we come to accept that our hands are empty, even if filled with the treasures of the world.

Accepting our poverty can lead to deep relaxation and peace. We can stop manipulating and varnishing our image and let our imperfections show. Paradoxically, when we accept the poverty of our personality, we can settle into the riches of true nature.

Realizing that we have nothing to give that spirit doesn't already have can also bring a greater appreciation of spirit itself. We see the overflowing fullness of Being, and it elicits our awe and gratitude. Knowing that spirit needs nothing from us frees us to be ourselves. We are not trying to earn what can't be earned. We are forced to recognize the gift nature of reality.

YIN MIND

Although a busy mind is one of the major hindrances to contemplative life, there are qualities of mind that can help enrich our life with spirit. I call these qualities *yin mind*, because they are yin characteristics according to the Chinese system. This is the mind that is open, empty, receptive, the mind that knows the power of inner space and is close to the Void and its mysteries. In the following verse, the word *heart* includes this yin aspect of mind.

> *Kneeling at the gates of Heaven,*
> *with only love to give,*
> *we listen for the rush of wings.*
> *Truth flies to the open heart.*

We learn in the verse that truth comes when we are open, unprejudiced. It is easier to maintain such openness when the mind is quiet. That is why inner silence is so important to contemplative life. We also learn from the verse that the self is kneeling, as a reflection of humility. We understand that we have much to learn and do not already know the answers.

Many of us have heard the Zen teaching story of the professor whose mind was too full to take in any more. The professor had gone to a Zen master, purportedly to learn from the sage, but he was full of his own learning and all he did was talk. The master asked if he wanted tea, and upon the man's acceptance, began pouring. He continued pouring the tea beyond the cup's capacity. The professor protested, noting that the cup was full. The master explained that, like the cup, a mind that is full cannot take more in. The professor would have to let go of his preconceptions and come back to "beginner's mind" if he was to learn.

It is not easy to keep an open mind when we have been filled with ideas and when pungent life experiences have led to strong convictions. It helps if we can stay curious and really want to know the truth. Then we are happy, whatever the outcome. Discovering reality must become more rewarding than confirming our beliefs. It may satisfy the mind to deal in the currency of ideas, but it satisfies the soul to meet the truth that is here in the moment.

Contemplation is being in the moment, meeting the truth, and the mind must take the yin position in this. The mind is not the arrow speeding toward the target; the mind is the target. Truth is the arrow that comes to it. Thus the mind is involved, but more in the way the fabric holds the dye. It becomes the medium through which something can reveal itself. An illumined mind is one in which truth is free to shine.

CONTEMPLATIVE READING AND WRITING

There has often been a place in religious life for reading sacred texts. Sometimes there are prescribed methods for doing this, such as *lectio divina*, a practice of listening to repeated readings of holy scripture from an open, receptive place. My own practice of contemplative reading developed quite spontaneously. I was not schooled in formal practices, nor were the materials I selected traditional holy books. They were simple notes taken from my favorite readings.

Approaching these in a contemplative way, I read these notes much as those who practice *lectio* read scripture. I listen from a place of inner silence, my heart open, receptive, inviting the words to illuminate me. I am not reading for information, for none of it is new. I read these words I have read many times before as a way of attuning to the reality they are talking about. I am feeling for that which lies beneath the words, the truth that words can only point to.

We can approach writing in a similar way. The posture is one of receptivity. We are not writing to show off what we know, but to learn. Thus we kneel in an attitude of prayer, feeling into the atmosphere of what is drawing near. We sense inwardly, groping for the words that best express that which is touching us. We let ourselves become saturated with an experience and articulate it through writing. Although the words are the end product, they are not the most important result. What is more important is that we are changed by what we experience. We are like a porous clay that takes on the colors of the liquids that pass through it. There is a vacuum-like action, our desire to feel and learn draws in the experience that can best teach us.

A contemplative approach to reading and writing thus hinges on receptivity. The more deeply we can take things in, the more the sacred can speak to us.

CONTEMPLATIVE LIVING

By now, you should be getting a feeling for the yin quality of contemplative life. You have read about the value of creating open space so things can come in, and of empty space where we rest and nurture what is ripening within us. You have read about waiting in silence with empty hands. In the next chapter, you will read more about abiding in a state of openness. The feminine quality of inclusiveness shows up in the *both/and* quality of embracing solitude *and* relationship, restraint *and* enjoyment. I hope you can feel the receptive, sensing quality inherent in contemplative reading and writing, as well as in the process of following one's experience which I describe later in chapter 10. In chapter 11, we find the yielding quality of the feminine when I talk about surrender and letting go of control. Chapter 13 contains some material about a return to embodiment and resacralizing the material world. In the last chapter, I write about the realm of mystery and include a poem about mystical union, written as a metaphor of a woman receiving her lover.

I point all of this out because I think it is this yin flavor that is the essence of contemplative life. You can't follow the flow if you are busy following your own agenda. You can't listen if you are like the professor, too full of your own knowing. You can't wait in silence with empty hands if you think you have to be somebody or do something. The way ("tao") of contemplation is much more about nondoing than it is about doing. This is a cornerstone of Taoist philosophy. Nondoing (wu-wei) is doing only those things that are natural and in alignment with the flow. It is action so in harmony with the Tao that it makes no waves and leaves no footprints.

chapter 9

Open Presence

No guards at the entrance
the palace is empty.
No position to defend
all become friends.

The palace in the above verse is a metaphor for the personality.
It is not empty in the literal sense, but the sovereign has departed; the ego-self is still. In this state, there is nothing to
defend, no one's honor to be spoiled. There is no fear of thieves,
for what is left cannot be stolen.

This verse tells us that the need to defend comes with the
ego. When the ego is inactive, we don't feel reactive. This is
quite different from the experience of our usual identity, which
feels it has much to lose, our sense of well-being and pride easily
shaken.

Daily life is full of assaults; we have to be able to tolerate a
little bruising. It helps to know that what is bruised is only a
small part of us. When we identify with our deeper nature, we
are not so disturbed by these things. I remember a time when
my pride was hurt by not having professional work. When I
could step away from my feelings of shame, I realized that it
really didn't matter what other people thought. Whatever
images were generated from seeing me in a menial job were
simply projections onto the outer surface of something. They
didn't touch the reality of me.

Do you see what I am driving at? It is the ego that feels fragile. As long as we are identified with this part of ourselves, we

will never feel that we're enough. Oh, it is true that this is usually hidden from view, but kick out a couple of supports and out it will come. The best defense is to get off the losing team. We must let go of our identity as ego. It does no good to hang my sense of self-esteem on a prestigious position. If I lose the position, I will quickly see that my sense of value is superficial. There is only one part of us that is free from insecurity, only one part that doesn't need bolstering or protection or defense. That is the part that can't be hurt. It is the inner nature of our being. The part that can never die.

BARRIERS TO OPENNESS

Being open means that we are not restricted. We are free enough of judgment and personal agenda to take in whatever is presented. We are like an open space without walls. There are no protections and no barriers.

It is obvious from the above discussion that this openness is obstructed by our ego needs and insecurities. By *ego needs*, I mean things like needing approval, needing to be right, wanting power, prestige, and attention. Can you see how these things make us more self-conscious and controlled? When we're wrapped up in our need for approval, we don't have much spontaneity. We're not free to be nobody and, thus, not free to be ourselves.

We are also restricted by our judgments about what is acceptable. It is hard to be friendly with all of our experience if we believe some of it is humiliating or shameful or wrong. You can explore this in the exercise on p. 72.

The wise person does not make unnecessary enemies by drawing unnecessary lines. Whenever you divide yourself from something or push against it, this creates a counterforce. Stop rejecting, and the enemy becomes a friend. If we can learn to

---

Exploration: *Who is the Enemy?*

Write down the qualities in yourself that you tend to reject. For example, you might note that you cut off your strength and ambition, your sexuality, your aggression. Anything you reject, you make into an enemy. These are the qualities you defend against in yourself and others. Now look at these qualities again. What makes them wrong? Can you see any similarity between what you reject in yourself and what was rejected in your early environment?

---

accept the rejected aspects of ourselves, they will lose much of their energy and will settle in and become an integrated part of our being.

It takes a while to make friends with these rejected parts. When I was first doing my healing work, I found it impossible to allow certain feelings. It wasn't just that they were unfamiliar; they were unacceptable to me. In time, I learned that it was valuable to allow every feeling, that each was necessary and each brought a gift. So, like the good student I am, I cried and raged and laughed, expressing the feelings I had denied. It is only re-cently that I recognized that the judgments are still there. I had confronted certain feelings with perhaps the same resoluteness with which I might take my medicine, but I had not embraced them. I didn't really love them or love myself for having them. So when I talk about the importance of accepting all the aspects of ourselves, I know personally how difficult this is.

It is not just prejudices against certain feelings or qualities that limit our openness, but also our beliefs about what is true. All beliefs limit us to some extent; the question is, how much?

This is determined somewhat by content, but more by how we hold our beliefs. It is only when we hold them loosely, suspending them at times, allowing our beliefs to be challenged, that we are open enough to discover something new. It goes back to the concept of beginner's mind. When we are new at something, we're very open to learning. It is when we think we already know, that we close.

Our openness can also be limited by deeply entrenched habits and routines. Our way of doing things can become so automatic that we are no longer present in the moment. If we're not present, we can't be open.

OPEN PRESENCE

There are various levels of presence. First, there is the obvious level that relates to physical presence. Either we're here, or we're not. Often, when we're talking about presence, it is something that is on a gradient; we are more present or less present depending on our attention. On this level, presence has to do with being emotionally and mentally available. Being present means you are right here experiencing whatever is happening. No part of you is turning away.

There is also a deeper level of presence where we become aware of the basic fabric of existence. This fabric itself is made of presence. It is the one element that cannot be reduced to anything else; its most fundamental quality is that it *is*. To our ordinary consciousness, it can appear somewhat paradoxical. Pure presence feels very light and yet it has a quality of being substantial; it feels empty, and, at the same time, full.

Thus, in the first kind of presence, I am fully here as my self, but in the deepest level of presence, what is here is pure being. It takes most people many years of work before they can consciously experience this. We must get beneath the noise and distinguishing characteristics of our personalities in order to sense what we are made of. Because this fabric is the ground of everything, our awareness of it grows when we stop experiencing through the lens of the individual self. This makes sense, if you think about it. A wave must let go of its identity as a wave in order to know itself as the ocean.

What allows us to be present at all of these levels (beyond the physical) is the quality of openness. We need to be open and undefended to be emotionally present, and it takes complete openness to fall into the openness and vulnerability that is our true nature.

So the words *open presence* fit together. These are the words used by author Gerald May to describe contemplation. He suggests that contemplative life is not withdrawing from the world but rather opening more deeply into present experience. What-ever practices we use for supporting this open presence should be as natural to us as possible.[1] I very much agree with him.

When we become an open presence, we can harmonize with life in a seamless way. We can feel the oneness behind things, and our actions can express this nonduality too. When we are really open and tuned in, experience and response become one process. Just as the sunflower turns toward the Sun in the act of sensing it, our actions become a natural response to what is being felt. We don't need to think about what to do; it is here, embedded in the moment.

---

1. Gerald G. May, *The Awakened Heart: Opening Yourself to the Love You Need* (San Francisco: HarperSanFrancisco, 1991).

Living with an Open Heart

Although I think open presence implies an open heart, there are a few things I want to say about the heart specifically. The heart is our place of feeling and of connecting with others. It is also the home of the divine. Having our hearts open is therefore important in being able to feel our emotions, love and empathize with others, and to perceive the God within. It is in the heart that we find the inner sanctum of the soul, described in the poem on page 76.

Exploration: *Open Presence*

Lie or sit in a comfortable position in an environment where you will not be disturbed. You may wish to put on some instrumental music, if that is soothing for you. Now, take yourself through a brief relaxation in which you consciously scan your body. Each time you encounter an area of contraction, breathe into it and see if you can let go. There is no need for muscles to be tight and on guard. Remind yourself that there is nothing to do, nowhere to go, nobody to be. You are simply here, as yourself. Let your body and mind be soft and permeable. Imagine love caressing you, your whole being opening up in response. Remain in this unguarded state for several minutes, breathing deeply and naturally.

This is an exercise that can be done again and again, daily if desired. It is a corrective to the time we spend curled in on ourselves, absorbed in self-concern. Relaxing and opening this way helps restore our more natural shape and makes us more sensitive to our essential nature.

Holy Presence

Deep within my heart
where only faith can go
lies a sacred chamber:
the inner sanctum of my soul.

It is the holy of holies
the place where the presence of God
is so absolute, so shattering,
no Other can remain.

Here, I am stripped bare,
all falsity and unworthiness burned away
by this scorching light
no darkness can withstand.

Shorn of self,
the distinctions *I*'s can see,
all that remains is the holy presence
the divine outpouring of itself.

The true communion
is not between a beggarly soul and God
but Truth with Truth
Light with Light,
the meeting of the Real
in what looked like two parts
now found to be one
sacred being
whose presence is everywhere.[2]

---

2. *Freefall to the Beloved: Mystical Poetry for God's Lovers* (Boulder, CO: Golden Reed, 1996), p. 62.

The poem suggests that the divine is not so much an entity as it is a radiant presence that is not bound by locality. The true communion comes when we relax into the fundamental ground that pervades everything.

We come to this ground by going within. The word "contemplate" is related to the word "temple," and we can think of contemplation as entering the inner temple. The tricky part is getting inside. We can't just push our way in, as we might push our way into the marketplace. The doors need to open to us. I think they open in response to our love, gratitude, sincerity, and surrender, and to our longing for God and for truth. They open more easily when the mind has become still.

In order to enter the inner sanctum, the heart must be open. Opening the heart is a matter of working through the layers of defense we have used to protect it. The coverings are the result of various hurts. As we move into the heart, we naturally rub up against them. To dissolve these layers of protection, we need to feel whatever it was that caused us to retract in the first place. If we can simply feel it, without evading or rejecting it, and without trying to make anything happen, we can metabolize the experience and we won't need the barrier anymore.

The exercise on p. 78 is designed to uncover some hurts and consequent fears that have caused you to close your heart.

Another thing that happens when the heart is open is that we feel the suffering of others more keenly. The Buddhists have a practice called *tonglen,* in which one breathes in suffering and breathes out love and healing. This cultivates compassion and helps soften the defensive boundaries that are so often present.

When the heart is supple and open, it doesn't take much to move us. A moment of need, an act of kindness, a baby animal—we are touched by many things. Life becomes sweet, even when there is sorrow, because our open heart makes it sweet.

Exploration: *Exploring Your Fears*

The best way to do this exercise is with a friend, but it is also possible to do it alone. This is a repeating question, which means that we ask the same question over and over in order to bring out as many responses as possible. The question is, "What is scary about living with an open heart?"

If you are doing the exercise with a partner, take ten minutes each to answer the question. The question is asked as many times as the time period allows. If you are the partner who is asking, your job is simply to ask the question, receive the response by saying "Thank you," or giving some kind of nonverbal acknowledgment, and then ask the question again. If you are the one who is answering, listen to the question and give a new response each time the question is asked. The response may be short or long. It's not necessary to explain things. This exercise is not about reporting what you know, but about feeling deeply and discovering what is true. This is also not the time to get into a dialogue; it's a time for each of you to explore your own experience. After ten minutes, switch roles.

If you are doing this alone, I suggest that you write the question on top of a sheet of paper and read it to yourself. Record your response below the question and then ask it again. You will end up with an interesting list to consider.

An exercise like this can help you look more objectively at some of your fears. Often they are based on past experiences. It is helpful to remember that you are no longer the same person, and you can handle more now.

open presence

It has been said that there is no greater teacher than living with an open heart. It is a source of wisdom and compassion, and it allows us to learn from the many painful and wonderful things that happen to us. The heart can guide us to our destination, because it knows the destination. It is the destination. It is the place we come to know the one sacred being whose presence is everywhere.

chapter 10

Healing Into
the Present Moment

Clearing away the old
the slate is scrubbed clean
leaving me here, in the moment,
a bright and shining now
where everything is alive
with magic.

As Gerald May has suggested, contemplation is about entering
fully into the present moment. Fortunately, there are a number
of spiritual practices that can help us do this. They are called by
different names, but they have a common strategy. The underlying principle seems to be that if you focus your attention on
sensing and feeling inwardly for the subtle perception of Being,
you won't be so caught in the tangled net of mind. It is thinking
that creates a veil over everything. Step away from thought, and
the world is alive, full of magic.

THE CASE FOR TRANSFORMATION

Many spiritual paths are about transcending the personal self
and leaping into another level of consciousness. I think it is
more helpful to transform, rather than transcend, the personality. I make two arguments for this. First, the personality is where
we live most of the time. Very few people have actually transcended it in any permanent way. (When I am speaking of the
personality here, I am referring to our usual cluster of likes and
dislikes, our attitudes and attachments, our idiosyncrasies and

adaptations.) We may experience moments when we drop the particulars and feel ourselves to be part of a larger current, but we come back. It is far nicer to come back to a place that has been renovated and cleaned up than to return to an old shack.

We have witnessed too many gurus who have reached what appear to be very high levels of consciousness, but whose unrefined cravings end up poisoning the very communities they have founded. They end up in sex scandals, shady financial dealings, and power trips because they haven't integrated and refined the parts of their personalities that can be caught in these traps. The path of transcendence is lined with potential dangers.

That's one argument for transformation over transcendence. Another is that most of us simply cannot make the leap. There are too many barriers. We are far too caught in our patterns to have the openness, clarity, or freedom to live in more refined states of consciousness. When we do the work needed to transform the personality, it becomes easier to make contact with essence and to do it more often, because we are closer to it. Thus, transforming the personality helps us move beyond it.

This is a therapeutic process; it is about healing. It is not quick or easy, but there are many helpers and rewards along the way. We can go to therapeutic bodyworkers to help clear the "issues in the tissues," the psychological contents now embedded in our physical structure. We can find courses or self-help groups to help us examine and release core beliefs that limit us. Psychotherapists can help us do the emotional work that is needed. We need to work through the contents of our personalities rather than simply sidestep them. Actually we need to do both: to see the familiar emotional dramas and not get caught in them, and to work through our most painful feelings so that these barriers to our clarity and freedom are burned away. We work with our feelings to heal the past. When we heal the past, it drops away as a formative influence and we are left right here, right now, experiencing the moment as it is.

Thus we go into ourselves so that we can outgrow ourselves. We give ourselves attention so that we may some day grow beyond the need for so much attention. We clear the body, mind, and emotions so that the qualities of our deeper nature can shine through.

FOLLOWING YOUR EXPERIENCE

Central to both the journey of self-actualization and the journey of Self-Realization is the ability to stay with our moment-to-moment experience. This ability to be with our experience is really a progressive deepening of the sensing process itself. Just as the process of contemplative writing is feeling into a content that can then be articulated, sensing our experience is a kind of *feeling into*—this time, into the contents of body, mind, and spirit.

Often we start by scanning our body for information, becoming ever more discriminating and sensitive as we practice this. For example, I become aware, not only of the pain in my hip, but of the fact that it starts with a tension in my back that has something to do with a fear of letting go of control. The same is true of feelings. I become aware, not just of the fact that I feel frisky, but of an irrepressible desire to not be contained, but to express myself freely and exuberantly. I can learn to follow any of these contents into deeper states of consciousness.

Gradually, inner senses may open, so that we see what the physical eyes cannot see, taste what is not in our mouths, and smell states of consciousness. I must say that I don't know many people who have opened up these inner senses. I mention it only to open your mind to the possibilities that exist. You don't really need to do anything more than to just stay with your experience in the way I have described.

I say "just" stay with your experience, but that is no small thing. It is a skill that develops with practice. Most of us need help honing it. Some people develop this skill through mindfulness meditation. They learn to sit with their experience, observing it carefully. I am more familiar with therapeutic processes where psychotherapists or other trained facilitators help clients pay attention to their immediate experience. In some therapies, creating this present-centered awareness is key. Once this state of consciousness is established, the work happens on its own. The therapist's job is to create a container and not interfere.

Creating a container means creating a safe space. This is both a physical and an emotional space. In therapy, the relationship is the primary container. It is imperative that clients experience their therapist as an ally who will do them no harm. They must be able to relax their defenses, so that whatever has been kept at bay can now emerge. In the field of psychotherapy, we say the therapist provides a "holding environment." Good friends can do this as well. When we share our ups and downs with our friends, they can help us "hold" the experience. Part of becoming more autonomous is learning how to hold our own experience, not so we won't need anyone else, but so we don't have to stop our process when we're alone. This involves both learning how to stay with the experience and knowing how to provide the safe container needed. Here are some things that have helped me.

The first has to do with the emotional space of the container. We must learn that we can trust ourselves, that we won't attack or reject our feelings, but will meet them with compassion. Working with a skilled therapist for a period of time can provide valuable modeling that we can later copy. I essentially internalized the woman who worked with me over a period of years and could easily imagine (and therefore replicate) her responses to my emerging experience. If you have a compassionate friend, you can imitate that person's responses. Another strategy is to imagine how God or your Higher Self might respond to your feelings. It is important that you meet your experience in a way that is accepting, so that it will continue to reveal itself.

The other element of the container is the physical surroundings. Although, ideally, we can contact our feelings even in hostile environments, it is much easier if we adapt our environment to make it more nurturing. When I am at home and I want to stay with difficult feelings, I lock the door, turn off the phone, reduce the surrounding noise in any way I can, and change the lighting. These are physical reminders that I have marked off this time and space for myself.

Another thing that has become an integral part of my process is working with my journal. This serves as an anchor by helping me recognize when I am skirting away from scary and painful states. The mind has many ways of distracting us. One is simply to turn our attention in another direction, be it a task or a daydream. A judgment can also serve as a distraction because it turns us away from the experience itself and enmeshes us in an evaluation of it instead. If I am judging my dependency, I am probably not really feeling it. We may also create substitute feelings or physical armoring to avoid sensitive emotions. We may, for example, tighten up or get angry in order to avoid feeling helpless. We have a lifetime's worth of practice in ways to step away from our immediate experience.

My journal helps me by holding the thread. I record my emerging experience and, when I find myself wandering away, I look back at what I had been feeling right before I wandered. The journal also holds my experience by giving me a place in which to express it. There are times when I leave the writing to cry or rage or immerse myself in an internal state, but I come back.

People sometimes talk about their journal as if it were an outside party, but really it is a vehicle that can be used to strengthen the relationship with yourself. It holds, mirrors, and amplifies your experience in a way that allows you to become more intimate with it. I think a journal is a valuable companion, both in the journey to find yourself and in the process of losing your self. I have used it for healing work and for anchoring me through subtle and not-so-subtle experiences where I have let go of my psychological structure and felt myself disperse.

This is where the two journeys come together. It is not that emotional experience limits us to the personal realm. Worked with in the right way, emotional experience becomes a gateway to the transpersonal. This requires being attuned to the deeper and subtler underpinnings of our experience. If we are too caught in the story, we don't feel this. If we don't know that these deeper and subtler dimensions exist, we won't look for them. The tools of most presence-centered or process-oriented psychotherapists are adequate for helping people on their spiritual journeys, but most therapists do not approach it in this way. If we can stay as interested in what happens after the catharsis as during it, as curious about who is having the experience as we are captured by the content, this will help us take the next step. Perhaps the biggest difference between spiritual guides and psychotherapists is that the guides have scouted out

Exploration: *Staying with Your Experience*

This exercise is practice in what can become an ongoing process of inquiry into your experience. You can do it with a trusted friend or by yourself. If you do it by yourself, I suggest you use a journal in the way described above. The exercise is to feel and name your experience for a set period of time—say twenty minutes. Keep it in the present tense and, as much as possible, include body sensations, thoughts, and feelings. Let the process of sensing guide your articulation. Feel inside for just the right word, and let the experience unfold. For example, what may start out as heaviness in the chest and an awareness of sadness, may become longing, or what may seem like a hard and unfeeling attitude may later be recognized as hatred. A contraction may open into spaciousness.

If you are doing this with a friend, speak your experience aloud. "Right now I am aware of tightness in my face. It feels as if my jaw is clenched and holding on to something. I feel like a dog holding onto a bone, not wanting to let go. That's how I feel in this relationship...."

Stay with the feelings in an open and curious way, trusting that whatever you need to know will become apparent. Perhaps a memory will surface or you will see a connection you hadn't recognized before. Imagery may arise from your unconscious. Let it all be there without making too much of it. Above all, don't *try* to make anything happen. The point is to stay in touch with what *is* happening.

the territory and can, therefore, recognize spiritual states as they arise. These states don't come with bells and whistles, so it is easy to look right past them. The teacher who recognizes the invisible states crossing our consciousness, can hold up a mirror and help us to recognize them as well.

I believe this one tool of following our experience can take us all the way. The Perennial Wisdom shining through every major spiritual tradition of the world tells us that, if we persistently look into our own experience, we will discover that who we are is not different or separate from what we call God, Cosmic Consciousness, the Tao, Nirvana and countless other names.[1]

NOW AND ZEN

I copied this name from Now & Zen, Inc., a manufacturing and publishing company in Boulder, Colorado. The phrase delights me, capturing for me the lively spirit of Zen Buddhism. Zen is now. There is no then.

Zen is about being awake. It is about perceiving reality directly without filtering it through the concepts of your mind. It is the mind that takes us out of the present. When mind is still, there's no place but here, no time but now—just life as it is, with nothing added. According to Charlotte Joko Beck, this is the essence of Zen. We leave the magical fantasies of the mind to come into the real magic of the moment.[2]

It takes us a while to get there. Joko (as she is called) explains that, for many years, practice serves to strengthen the observer. This makes sense from my perspective as a psychotherapist because observing is a way to not be totally identified with an experience and thus tolerate it without being

---

1. Duane Elgin, *Voluntary Simplicity: Toward a Way of Life that Is Outwardly Simple, Inwardly Rich* (New York: William Morrow, 1993), p. 134.
2. Charlotte Joko Beck, *Nothing Special: Living Zen* (San Francisco: HarperSan-Francisco, 1993).

overwhelmed. In time, we don't need this stepping-away as much. We can experience more directly. Joko describes this as being willing to meet whatever is there without the observer.[3]

This experiencing-without-labels is described beautifully by Toni Packer, a former Zen teacher who has moved beyond the formal aspects of Zen and now directs the Springwater Center for Meditative Inquiry in New York. Toni never tires of reminding people of the importance of being in touch with our immediate experience without any need to describe or analyze it. At times she calls this "seeing"; at other times she describes it as "listening."[4] In a sense, it is experiencing without the mind, without the need to recognize or understand.

This makes it a little different from the process I described above. I can imagine the two as different points on a continuum. Just as witnessing gives way to raw experience, naming gives way to wordless recognition. If you don't quite get this, that's fine. Don't worry about the distinctions, or where you are on the continuum. The point is to stay as close to your experience as possible, close to what actually is. Only then can we know reality.

---

3. Charlotte Joko Beck, *Nothing Special: Living Zen*, p. 27.
4. Toni Packer, *The Light of Discovery* (Boston: Tuttle, 1995).

chapter 11
Letting Go

No ripples on the surface
only the current moves.
No self to resist
only the Tao acts.

One of the biggest lessons in spiritual work is learning how to let go. This shouldn't surprise you, given how much I have emphasized the need for openness and receptivity. We can't wait with empty hands if we are still holding on to anything.

In the process of Self-Realization, there are moments when it seems that everything must go. I have felt this acutely at times, and it can be rather frightening. Only later have I realized that letting go doesn't mean that everything disappears. Some things disappear (certain ideas and self-images for example) and others remain, minus our efforts and our attachments. Just as I can let go in my body, and that doesn't mean that my body disappears, I can let my identity shatter and find that I am still here. In a similar way, I can stop holding on to someone in an important relationship, letting go of my hopes and agendas, and that doesn't mean that the relationship ends. The relationship continues as it is, minus everything I have added to it. What goes away is the "stuff" in our minds, the familiar way of holding something.

Since what we are letting go of has actually been limiting us, what we gain is very much worth gaining. When we let go of thinking, for example, we discover the sky-like quality of the mind. When we let go of our preconceptions and ideas, we experience how things actually are. When we surrender the pattern we are trying to impose on our lives, we can better feel the shape they are trying to take. We can move in harmony with the Tao.

LETTING GO OF CONTROL

Have you ever wondered why life involves so much struggle? Usually, we assume this is just the way things are, that we are struggling against the contingencies of the world in order that we may survive and thrive. But perhaps this is true only because of how we interact with the world. Some say that the struggle comes from not going with the flow. The struggle comes with trying to fit a square peg into a round hole, trying to make things be other than the way they are. Our efforts to manipulate and control make us adversaries with reality.

To let go and simply "go with the flow" is not easy. It feels threatening to the ego-self whose existence is based on creating its own pattern. To go with the flow erases this pattern and the sense of self associated with it. When we are really going with the flow, there is just flow, without a "me."

The need to be in control develops early in life as a protection against feelings of helplessness and the harm associated with others having control. We mistakenly conclude that if we can keep control, bad things will not happen. For those who grow up in really unstable environments, keeping control can seem like a matter of life and death.

Control is not only linked to safety; it has many other positive reinforcers. After all, being in charge often leads to desired results. We get what we want, and we feel stronger for it. We feel more solid and substantial because we have had an effect. This all makes sense from the perspective of ordinary consciousness and our everyday lives. It is useful to have a strong ego and to be able to successfully negotiate in the world. The problem is that it becomes hard to let go of this initiating, steering self. If we want to know ultimate reality, we must let go. Facing our fears can help ease the way.

> Exploration: *What Might Happen?*
>
> Write this question at the top of a sheet of paper and then answer it as many times as you can. *What might happen if I let go of control?*

Usually our first response to an exercise like this reveals our fears. Examined carefully, we see that most of these fears are not very objective. They are exaggerated, worst-case scenarios. If you persist long enough in the exercise, you may come to some potentially enjoyable possibilities. You may see that let-ting go of control can lead to more relaxation, a more carefree attitude, more friendliness toward others, and greater intimacy.

FREEFALL

In almost every situation where we are holding on to something, fear is operating. This is true whether we are talking about letting go of job, a career path, a relationship, a self-image, or even relaxing deep holding patterns in our musculature. When we are challenged to let go of the ego structure itself, tremen-dous fears arise. We don't know what can possibly hold us together, how we can survive, who will take care of us, or whether we will even continue to exist.

To the extent that our fears go unchallenged, they reign supreme. We don't learn that the disastrous consequences we so vividly imagine will not happen, because we don't put ourselves in a situation in which we can find out. We simply hold on until we no longer can. Only then do we find what is holding us. The following poem describes this experience.

Freefall to the Beloved

I.   Hands cramp, clutching tightly,
desperate to hold on.
I am afraid to let go,
afraid of plummeting to my death.
Panic seizes me as I realize
I cannot do this much longer.
My grasp is slipping.

II.   I am falling,
falling through space.
Ah, what freedom!
What absolute freedom!
There is no drag, nothing to hold me back.
The farther I fall, the faster I fall,
dizzy with the pleasure.

III.   It is over now,
the ground safely beneath me,
a holy, loving ground
that would never let me be hurt.
The Beloved was watching all along,
eager for the fall,
so that I could know these loving arms
here from the beginning.

Freefall to the Beloved—
Why wait?[1]

---

1. Jasmin Cori, *Freefall to the Beloved: Mystical Poetry for God's Lovers* (Boulder, CO: Golden Reed, 1996), p. 94.

letting go

It is only after we let go that we see there was no danger. Before that, we hold on for dear life. This holding on is instinctive and hard to override. It helps if we can trust. I think of faith as being independent of experience and trust as something that can develop through experience. Let me share a story about how trust developed for me.

Several years ago, I was at a crossroad. I had been teaching in colleges and professional schools for many years and felt intuitively that it was time for a change, but I was afraid to let go. What I really wanted to do was write, but I didn't see how I could support myself. I ignored my misgivings and hung on to the job, jumping at a promotion in the hope that it would give me new life. I got the promotion, but shortly thereafter, I took a political stand and was fired. I took up my writing in earnest then, but still felt insecure about money. Every time I tried to go back to the kinds of work that had provided security in the past, I got nowhere. I worried a lot, but the writing kept coming. Finally, I had to admit that when I gave myself completely to writing, I had whatever financial resources I needed. The numbers didn't make sense, but when I accepted the miraculous nature of it, I couldn't deny the trustworthiness of the result. Mine was a case of getting hit with the cosmic two-by-four and learning by experience. I didn't have the faith and foresight to let go gracefully.

This is just one area of my life. Through many years of doing deep spiritual work, I came to realize that all of my attempts to hold on were simply my resistance to the natural unfoldment of things. On one level, this holding on can slow things down; on another, it really has little effect. Things will happen as they will, despite everything. I came to understand that trying to control the unfoldment of things was as silly as a wave in the ocean having its own agenda, or a leaf on a tree planning when it will fall in the autumn. Control is ultimately an illusion that holds the trying self in shape.

As we see in the above poem, it is only when we stop trying to provide safety and security for ourselves that we recognize that something larger is holding us, watching over us, guiding us. This may be conceptualized in different ways. It might be as a guardian angel, God, our Higher Self, or our own essence. We feel it when we let go and allow ourselves to be carried by the current of grace that is streaming through our lives.

Exploration: *The Current*

There are several options for this exercise. If you can lie or sit next to a stream—somewhere peaceful—that is ideal. Another good option is to create a comfortable environment in which you won't be disturbed and put on environmental music that incorporates the sounds of running water. Relax and imagine yourself carried by the current. You may visualize yourself as a particular form at first—a person, leaf, or any other object—but, at some point, let go of that and just feel the current itself. Let yourself become the current.

MOVING WITH THE TAO

Let's return to this chapter's opening verse. *No ripple on the surface, only the current moves. No self to resist, only the Tao acts.* What this verse is saying is that there is action even when there is not a self initiating it. In fact, our action will feel more natural and effortless when there is no self to struggle, no resistance to overcome. We simply do what needs to be done.

Ego cannot imagine this. It suffers from the delusion that if it were to stop acting, nothing would ever get done. This is not true. The person who is permeable to Being continues to take action—skillful, constructive action that simply feels like "the right thing to do." It feels like the right thing because it is in harmony with the Tao and because it is actually the Tao that is moving through us.

We can experience this in little ways and in big ways. We may do something that seems totally insignificant, only to find that our small action was like the right piece at the right time in a much larger puzzle. Many have written about this from the perspective of synchronicity, the meaningful coincidences that suggest something different from our usual picture of causality. Although such coincidences may seem extraordinary in our ordinary frame of reference, they do not seem so mysterious from the perspective of a unified whole. When something is happening in a field of being, the whole field participates.

When we really align with the flow of the Tao, we put ourselves in the service of what is sometimes referred to as Universal Will. We empty ourselves of our personal agendas and say to the intelligence that is running through life, "Use me as you wish." Although we must be willing to do anything, the situation is more harmonious than we might fear. The Tao is intelligent. It doesn't make sense in the economy of things to put people in positions for which they are not suited. The Tao utilizes our natural talents and inclinations. Often, what we love most points the way to how we can best be used. Thus, our own deepest desires and inclinations are in harmony with the Tao. In other words, we discover God's Will when we look deeply into our own hearts.

Making ourselves available like this doesn't mean that we get what we might consider to be one of the leading roles. We may not be one of those people who affect the life of the larger society in obvious ways. It is inappropriate to judge the value of our lives by how big they look. A life that may look inconsequential may have profound impact in ways that we will never see. We need to let go of our judgments and find out what is here, embedded in our hearts, revealed in the emerging flow of experience. Only then will we discover what is being asked of us.

Once when I was feeling my devotion to the truth, a critical part of me asked (with a sneer) just what I planned to do with the truth. I realized that the real question was: What does the truth want to do with me? This is the question we must stay with. What does God (or the Tao) want from me? How do I know what this is? How do I feel it? This is not a question that is answered once, but one that is continually asked and continually answered. In the end, if we have listened sincerely, we discover the answer in the pattern of our life.

We may also come to understand that it is not just what we do, but how we do it that is important. As Mother Teresa has noted, doing small things with great love is more important than doing great things with little love. If we do even the most magnanimous of things, but hold back part of our heart, we block the real opportunity. It is the whole-heartedness of our giving that opens the door for grace to work. When we give everything, there is nothing left to interfere with what God wants to accomplish through us.

Becoming a vessel in this way comes with deep surrender. It is a surrender that happens far from the place where we all begin. There are many little surrenders that precede this. We surrender again and again, until it becomes a continuous flow, and there is nothing but surrender.

chapter 12

Self Dissolves

Letting go of images
the pattern disappears,
self dissolving into no-self.
We lose nothing that's real.

Spiritual teachings often tell us that the self we usually identify with is not ultimately real. Liberation comes when we see through the illusion. It is a long process, in which we let go of one perspective to develop another. It is like giving up our eyes for the sake of developing our other senses. In this case, however, we give up our "I" to develop the capacity to experience Being.

Naturally, this changes not only *how* we perceive, but *what* we perceive. When we shift away from our usual point of view to a subatomic point of view, for example, discrete objects disappear. In a similar way, when we look from the perspective of Being, the world appears as a play of light. It is one fundamental nature shapeshifting into the world of manifestation, the Tao coming into form. To see it, we must change our perspective. We must change who is looking.

What Is the Self?

While exploring this question one day, I thought of the constellations in the night sky and realized that what we see as a distinctive thing is only an imposed pattern. The sky is strewn with stars forming myriad patterns from different angles. A constellation is merely a product of perception.

It is the same with the self. The self is a constellation of mental images, feelings, and body sensations woven into a unified experience we perceive as real and substantial. We say, "I am this person, in this body, with a particular history, a continuity of memory, a sense of volition, and an inner feeling of 'me.' What is there to question?"

My answer is that we should question the relationship between these components and the inner sense of "me." There is, in fact, a human being with a particular history; this is not an illusion. But the inner sense of "me" that seems so distinct and solid is not the same as the human person. The subjective self is usually quite out-of-date and lopsided. Certain experiences are overrated and others not included at all. Our sense of self is actually a construct built around a few key memories that act as a filter, allowing in only those additional experiences that are in line with it. Experiences that are not in line are generally excluded. In psychological language, they become the shadow, the unseen parts.

The shadow is a reminder that this cookie-cutter construct of self is not the whole picture. It is simply one form which the malleable substance of our being can take. Our true nature shares the shapeshifting quality of the Tao because it is the same nature. It is the same substance. Just as snowflakes are all made out of the same stuff, we are made of the same underlying nature.

It makes sense, then, that coming back to this more fluid nature opens up a much wider range of experiences and behaviors. When we stop identifying with the self, we stop knowing ourselves through exclusion. We put down the cookie cutter and let the dough come out however it wants to.

Usually we don't challenge our commonsense experience of self. Often it is only after we have experiences that fall outside the usual paradigm that we question what is real.

Exploration: *Beneath the Surface*

This is an exercise that can be done at home or out in nature. It is best if you can move around and touch the things you see. Each time you touch something, ask: "What lies beneath the surface?" Rather than think in purely physical terms, imagine the physical appearance as only the top layer. Do this for as long as you want. If you are really adventurous, do it until the process comes to a natural end.

I will not say what you should experience; there are many possibilities. You may become aware of a dimension of space pervading everything, or consciousness, or some kind of presence. The point is to open yourself to feel something deeper than the surface characteristics.

This questioning can lead to the kind of deconstructing experience that many people first discovered under the influence of psychedelic drugs. Any time we experience reality with something other than our pre-programmed minds, it is going to be different. Usually, this involves an altered state of consciousness, whether facilitated by drugs, natural circumstances, or spiritual practices. Such experiences dissolve the hold our programming has on us. We are then free to experience reality as it is—which some call enlightenment.

RECOGNIZING THE LIGHT

No one gets enlightened overnight. Yes, the shift in consciousness away from the subjective self can happen suddenly, but to not immediately snap back into our usual identity requires that significant changes have taken place. It has to be all right with us to be without that which we thought we were. We have to be able to feel ourselves exist even when there doesn't seem to be a being who exists. We have to be able to tolerate the brightness and fullness of true nature and the absence of our conceptual mind. We have to be able to simply be, without trying to be something.

All of these are hurdles, but the major one is simply letting go of the familiar structure of the self. The situation reminds me of being on a ropes course, where you stand on a high platform with an instructor telling you to jump. Your eyes say, "That's crazy. It's too far." And it may, indeed, be farther than you can safely jump—except for the fact that you are held by a set of ropes that won't let you fall. In order to leap, you have to remember the ropes and override your natural fear.

From where we usually stand, letting go of the self looks as terrifying as leaping off that platform. In order to leap, we have to remember that the situation is not as it appears. This is where spiritual teachings can play an important role. They provide us with reassurance, telling us that we will be all right. The teachings give us confidence, and that confidence may give us enough trust to let go.

Sometimes our spiritual teachers will give us a push. They may, for example, confront us with the insubstantiality of the self we are clinging to. The timing here is critical. Only when we are really close to our larger being can we tolerate such a challenge without needing to defend. At most other times, such a confrontation would feel like an assault. Tell the ego it is nothing, and it will react, either by jumping up in defense to say, "I am too something! I'll make you see how important and valuable I am!" or by solidifying into an identity of not being good enough. In either case, the ego becomes harder rather than softer. On the other hand, just the right push at the right time can help the ripened soul see itself more clearly. It can break the identification with our usual identity so that we recognize our larger being.

Many voices in transpersonal psychology tell us that it takes a healthy ego to be able to let go like this. The wounded self must first be healed. We must feel as if we are somebody before we are willing to be nobody. Until then, the ego is too defended to let itself dissolve. It may expand to include certain spiritual experiences, but it will do so in a way that distorts them.

Were we to jettison ego altogether (in permanent Self-Realization), it might not be so important to heal the personality, but this is rarely the case. We are lucky if we can leave it for even a moment. What we need is the flexibility that comes with a healthy structure and allows us to shift back and forth between ego and the larger Being.

Rather than demean the ego with the message that it is nothing, it might be better to say, "Yes, you are precious! I see the light in you." This helps the ego relax, because it feels seen. Actually, it is not ego itself that is supported here, but what is more real. Here is an analogy. If we were to compare a person to a light bulb, we would see that true nature is the light, the person is the bulb, and the ego identity is the print on the bulb. It is the little ID tag that says "General Electric." The goal of spiritual work is to get beyond the label and recognize the light.

When we do finally recognize the dimension of Being, we see that it is not limited to our physical person and is not a product of incidentals. Being is the ground; Being is what we're made of. When we don't recognize Being, we think that we are our bodies. We confuse the subjective feeling of "me" with the actual person. When that subjective feeling of "me" wavers because the structure of the self is dissolving, it feels as if we're going to disappear. We believe the death of the "I" is the end of all experience. But there is experience without an "I," just as there seems to be substantial evidence that there is experience without a body. Those who have reached the state of no-self can tell us something about it.

THE EXPERIENCE OF NO-SELF

The contemporary Christian contemplative Bernadette Roberts has described the experience of no-self in her books.[1] She describes how it felt to her from the inside and how it appeared to others not in this state. According to her reports, people didn't recognize anything different. She did not seem bewildered or otherwise changed. In fact, no one seemed to notice.

For Bernadette Roberts, the state of no-self was rather unspectacular. She didn't dissolve in bliss, but functioned efficiently with a practical, now-focused "thinking" that served her well. At first, she was aware that the usual self was gone, its habitual activity replaced by silence. Later, even this distinction faded from view.

Others tell a similar story. It is really not difficult to function without the ego-self. It is a relief not to have all the "stuff" that comes with it: the insecurities, the comparisons, the constant striving to be somebody, the reactions, the commentary, the maneuvering, and the push and pull of desire and aversion. Wouldn't it be a relief to be without all that?

The surrender of the separate self described by mystics through all time is really the dissolution of an imposed pattern. It is the beginning, not the end, of a deeper experience.

RESTING IN EMPTINESS

When the self first dissolves, what we usually find in its place is emptiness. It is not a painful emptiness, but a peaceful and

---

1. Bernadette Roberts, *The Path to No-Self* (Boston: Shambhala, 1991) and *The Experience of No-Self* (Boston: Shambhala, 1993).

pristine emptiness that reminds me of a field covered with freshly fallen snow. There is no one to leave a trail, no one tramping around making tracks. It sparkles in its purity.

We may have had experiences we would describe in terms of emptiness before this, but I would call these experiences of deficient emptiness.[2] This deficient emptiness can take many forms. One is that awful, gnawing sense of something missing, of life not holding enough meaning. Another comes when we feel deflated; the world does not support our self-image and we take it personally, concluding that something is wrong with us. We feel that our very being is deficient in some way, which is what the sense of shame refers to. At other times, disappointment is the doorway. We reach a goal, only to find out that it does not satisfy. All of these experiences can lead to the feeling of emptiness, but it is not a true emptiness, because it is not really empty. It is a painful psychological affect.

When we learn how to work with it, deficient emptiness can transform into something sweet and restful.[3] We can accept our feelings without identifying with them, and we can watch them transform. Allowing the emptiness to be there without judgment or reaction will bring out its deeper aspects. True emptiness, as I've said, is very peaceful. It is incredibly light and delicate. It is hard for the mind to exist in this emptiness,

---

2. I am indebted to The Diamond Approach for my understanding of deficient emptiness. See A. H. Almaas, *Diamond Heart, Book One* (Berkeley: Diamond Books, 1987).

3. This transformation of the emptiness is described not only in The Diamond Approach, but also in other places. One reads of it in the channeled work of Eva Pierrakos, such as *The Pathwork of Self-Transformation* (New York: Bantam Books,1990), and in Irena Tweedie's autobiographical account, *Daughter of Fire: A Diary of a Spiritual Training with a Sufi Master* (Inverness, CA: The Golden Sufi Center, 1986).

because the mind seems to need something to focus on and there is nothing there. And yet, paradoxically, there is holiness there. Emptiness is like a holy night waiting for something to be born. It is a holy nothingness, a holy absence, the holy womb of God.

This sweet and silent emptiness is more like the nature of God than anything we can point to. Coming to know and appreciate it is thus an important part of contemplative life.

chapter 13

The Way of Love

Tenderly, Love calls me
into intimacies beyond any I have known,
changing me in ways I cannot control,
leaving me vulnerable and open
a begging heart
good for only love.

Love is the great elixir, the agent of our transformation. It is love that fuels the search, love that dissolves us into itself, and love which, in the end, acts through us. How can we say that the spiritual journey is other than a path of love?

THE LOVERS OF GOD

The way of love doesn't belong to any one religion, for, as Rumi noted, lovers have a religion all their own. And yet the path that embodies it the most for me is the Sufi path, and the writer whose words most tenderly and passionately express it are those of contemporary Sufi teacher Llwellyn Vaughan-Lee. He writes of God as a lover would.

Sufis have sometimes been called the "lovers of God." The path, at least in some sects of this mystical branch of Islam, is depicted as a love affair. God is the Beloved who plants in us a deep and urgent need for Him. Actually this longing is our salvation, for it is our longing that draws us nearer; it is our longing that melts our defenses and structures, leaving us naked in the arms of the Beloved.

The Sufis have an interesting concept of staying sober while drunk on the wine of the Beloved. This means that the wayfarer continues to function in the world, while immersed in states of inner ecstasy. The longing, intoxication, surrender, and fidelity of the lover are themes found in mystical poetry. The following poem captures the desperate quality of the lover who will do anything to be united with the Beloved.

Reunion

I run to you
throwing myself at your feet
shattering into a thousand pieces
all for the love of you.

You *must* have me!
Oh, Beloved, do not turn your back!
I cannot bear to be apart from you,
cannot endure
anything less than my erasure,
any trace of our difference
a jabbing reminder
that I have failed.

Accept my love
or I will drown
submerged in its depths.
Is that what you want?
Must I drown in this love
to come home to you?
I will do whatever it takes—
shatter, drown, *anything*
to be with you.

I feel you now,
your arms around me
as you whisper in my ear
that you, too, have been waiting
for love to deliver me
whenever I was willing
to give everything
for the sake of our reunion.

Bless this moment![1]

For the lover, no sacrifice is too great. Lovers will give anything to end the separation that feels so unbearable. Their longing draws them nearer and nearer, like a moth to the flame, until the separating boundary is melted and they are absorbed into the Beloved, living in a state of union.

The above poem has an interesting twist. It is the willingness to give that opens the heart to the presence that is always here. This echoes the earlier poem, "Freefall," in which the Beloved also waits. It is a consistent theme: mystical union is not something we acquire, but something we open to. Despite the dramatic language of self-immolation and sacrifice I have used in my poetry, my own experience is that union is not something we fling ourselves into as much as something we relax into, like a droplet allowing itself to be absorbed by a larger drop.

Love is the magical elixir. According to Vaughan-Lee, it is the energy of love that slows the mind until it becomes empty and silent.[2] And it is through silence that we come into direct

---

1. Jasmin Cori, *Freefall to the Beloved: Mystical Poetry for God's Lovers* (Boulder, CO: Golden Reed, 1996), p. 26.
2. Llewellyn Vaughan-Lee, *The Call and the Echo* (Putney, VT: Threshold Books, 1992), p. 3.

contact with what is. Many everyday mystics (of whatever persuasion) have directly perceived that love is the fundamental medium from which everything is made. The world is nothing but a sea of love, expressed in every color and shape imaginable. The lover lives within this vibration.

REMEMBRANCE

The lovers of God have a personal relationship with the divine. It is the central, consuming relationship of their lives. One example of this is Brother Lawrence, a 17th-century Carmelite monk who spent the last forty years of his life continuously "practicing the presence of God."[3] For Brother Lawrence, this involved a continual awareness of God and an ongoing conversation with Him. He was always leaning into God's presence, always feeling for Him. His whole life became a process of remembrance. Everything Brother Lawrence did, he offered to God, and he was blessed with seeing God's presence everywhere.

Obviously, there is much more than technique or practice going on here. This kind of devotion comes from the heart that is consumed with love..Nonetheless, there are things that Brother Lawrence did that supported his relationship with God, and there are practices we can use to support remembrance.One that is found in various traditions is called *japa* or *dhikr*, or the prayer of the heart. This practice consists of a continual repetition of a sacred word or phrase; in the Sufi tradition, *dhikr*, it is often one of the names or attributes of God. At first, this repetition is conscious and voluntary, then it takes hold in the heart and continues on its own. The Sufis say that first you do the *dhikr*,

---

3. Brother Lawrence, *The Practice of the Presence of God* (New York: Doubleday, 1977).

and then the *dhikr* does you. It tunes you into the frequency of that sacred word and invokes the direct presence of God.

The only *dhikrs* I have practiced have been those put to music and made into dances as part of the Dances of Universal Peace. This is obviously much more active than the silent *dhikr*, and it engages the person on many levels. In this practice, you still the mind by moving the body. I find that the *dhikr* is a form that can hold me, while I sink down into a deeper level of the formless.

A friend of mine likes singing a *dhikr* for a period of time while hiking. It attunes her to the dimension of God; then, when she stops singing and just experiences the natural world around her, she finds herself exquisitely sensitive to God's presence. The *dhikr* stops the normal mind and prepares the ground for a deeper perception.

This same friend also uses the *dhikr* (as practiced in the Dances of Universal Peace) as a context for the inner work of transformation. She brings an issue to the *dhikr* and then surrenders it, letting it cook in the transformative energy generated by the group. Just as people bring to God their resistances to God, she brings to the *dhikr* the barriers that keep her from remembering her oneness with God, which is what *dhikr* is about.

Gerald May gives instruction on the prayer of the heart (the equivalent of *dhikr*) in his book, *The Awakened Heart*.[4] He also gives a number of practical suggestions for cultivating remembrance. They are simple little things that anyone can do. Yet the process is more than conscious, I believe. Llewellyn Vaughan-Lee writes about remembrance as something that grows within us as we progress along the path. It starts, not with our *attempts*

---

4. Gerald G. May, *The Awakened Heart: Opening Yourself to the Love You Need* (San Francisco: HarperSanFrancisco, 1991).

to remember, but with the actual remembering of a time when we were together with God.[5] This memory is planted deep within what the Sufis call the "heart of the heart." The memory pulls us along, slowly surfacing until the sense of this togetherness becomes an integral part of everyday life.

Like everything else, I think our ways of remembering should be as natural to us as possible. As May says, the best prayer is the one deep inside you that has been going on all along.[6] Our task is to find it.

LOVING GOD'S MANY FACES

Sufi teacher Atum Thomas O'Kane says that the Beloved comes to us through all that we love. We should therefore be attentive to those places where our heart responds deeply, for that is where the Beloved is. We must honor both the essence that is coming through and the forms through which it expresses itself.[7]

This is quite different from the split between spirit and matter common to most of our thinking and supported by most of our religions. Author and scholar Andrew Harvey believes that all of the major religions have in some way failed us in their overemphasis on the transcendent and their consequent loss of the Mother aspect of God. The Divine Mother is the universe and all things in it. She is both beyond and within everything. What we need now more than anything else is a return to the Mother.[8]

---

5. Llewellyn Vaughan-Lee, *In the Company of Friends* (Inverness, CA: The Golden Sufi Center, 1994), p. 26.

6. Gerald May, *The Awakened Heart: Opening Yourself to the Love You Need*, p. 161.

7. Workshop with O'Kane in Boulder, CO, May 1998.

8. Andrew Harvey, *The Return of the Mother* (Berkeley: Frog, 1995).

In other words, the form and the formless are two sides of the same coin. Matter is not separate from Being except in our minds, conditioned as they are to perceive a world of objects separate from the streaming. How did this happen? It is a complex subject, but here is a short version of it.

The object world is the world of objects that exists in our minds. It is built of concepts and shaped by language. It begins with parents pointing to part of the human face and saying, "nose," or pointing to a fragrant burst of red and saying, "flower." During this same time, the child is learning to create a concept of himself. Gradually this world of concepts becomes stronger than the world of actual experience.

To experience things as they actually are, we must step out of this fabricated reality. In the words of Carlos Casteneda's Yaqui sorcerer, Don Juan, we must "stop the world." We must stop the conceptualizing mind, stop naming things. We must let the outlines blur, the objects disappear, so that we see the magical shapeshifter dancing everything into existence. This is our entrance into the dynamic, unnamed flow of being.

This is one way to talk about it. We can deconstruct the object world by deconstructing the way we think and therefore perceive. Some people don't need to deconstruct the world to see spirit, because they never took spirit out of it. This is true of most native peoples. To see God in the material realm is a natural part of their experience.

It is here, in the so-called advanced cultures, that we have lost our perception of wholeness. Some are coming back to it through a reverence for creation and the incredible precision that creates and sustains life. Take, for example, the fact that four billion years ago the Earth had to maintain a temperature within a range of a few degrees or the oceans would either have evaporated or frozen, making it impossible for life to exist here.

As Matthew Fox, proponent of creation-centered spirituality says, "When you learn these truths and facts about our universe, you're just in awe about the gift of our being here."[9] This sparkling and alive universe can't be other than the work of a divine intelligence. The nature of creation is not other than that of the creator. Many of our most brilliant scientists are saying something similar in their own language.

I hope that one day we will more fully release our constructs of the world and reenter its mystery, learning to recognize and love God's many faces.

PRAISE AND THANKSGIVING

When we see the sacred all around us, our natural response is one of praise and thanksgiving. It engenders an attitude of gratitude. This gratitude opens our hearts even more.

Many popular books today give instructions and reminders for cultivating gratitude. People are encouraged to consciously say "thank you" for the many blessings they encounter each day. In some variations, the assignment is to give thanks for a particular number of events each day. Obviously, trying to rack up a certain number helps us notice and remember them, but the recitation is secondary. It is a good thing to actually say thank you, but what is really important is to cultivate the heart in such a way that we naturally feel appreciation all the time because we experience everything in such a sweet and intimate way. A person with a tender heart can be moved to tears by the smallest act of kindness. When the heart is sensitive like this, we are always saying thank you.

---

9. Matthew Fox interviewd by Michael Toms in *At the Leading Edge* (Burdette, NY: Larson Publications, 1991), p. 38.

Spiritual practices can help us come to this place. This is my favorite ritual of thanks-giving. It is a great one for Thanksgiving Day, but it can be done any time.

Exploration: *Thanksgiving Ritual*

More than any other exercise in this book, this one most needs to be done with other people. Ideally, it is done in a group. Several variations are possible; adapt it to suit you. The main point is to share gratitude in a way that is deep and heartfelt. I suggest sitting in a circle with candles and whatever else supports an intimate atmosphere. You can use a talking stick if you want to do it Native American style. I prefer using small, natural objects in plentiful supply. The last time I did it, we used chestnuts. As you go around the circle, each person says something he or she is thankful for and places one item in a basket or other appropriate receptacle. This continues for some time. With each turn, the person settles in and, as gratitude arises, says, "Thank you for _____ " [naming whatever it is]. When you run out of things to name, you simply say, "Thank you." When that "Thank You" travels around the circle without anyone adding something new, the exercise is over.

The process could take a couple hours, depending on the number of people involved. During this time, we marinate in gratitude, immersing ourselves completely. Gratitude is a form of love, and when it wells up from the heart, it is a very rich and fulfilling experience. So rich and so filling that it puts even pumpkin pie to shame. What a feast!

Gratitude also grows as we let go of our sense of entitlement and our attachment to things going the way we want them to go. Why should reality conform to our desires? It is our belief that it should that is the cause of suffering, according to Charlotte Joko Beck. In *Everyday Zen*, she talks about how we feel entitled not to have to go through pain.[10] This flies in the face of truth, because life is full of pain. Once we stop fighting reality, our appreciation can blossom.

Appreciation can also take the form of praise. Praise is simply an expression of adoration. There are songs and prayers of praise, poems and sermons overflowing with praise. The problem is that we put much more of our energy into appraising than we put into praising. We are always evaluating things, seeing how they measure up against some standard. I think the deepest praise comes when we stop looking through the critical eyes of the mind and look through the eyes of the heart. Then we behold the real majesty and can't help but bow down in honor.

LOVE IN ACTION

When your heart is open, you naturally want to reach out and help others. There are different ways people talk about this. Some describe it as serving God in others, while other people say that it is God who is serving through us. Mother Teresa combined these when she spoke of doing the work of Jesus for Jesus to Jesus.[11]

The natural response of the heart when it sees pain is compassion; service is simply acting on that compassion.

---

10. Charlotte Joko Beck, *Everyday Zen: Love and Work* (San Francisco: HarperSanFrancisco, 1989), p. 40.
11. Mother Teresa and Lucina Vardy (compiler), *A Simple Path* (New York: Ballantine, 1995).

Additionally, when you see that separating boundaries are not ultimately real and that we're all cells of one organism, it doesn't make sense to limit our concern to our narrowly defined self-interests. The ecological crisis is teaching us that in an interdependent world, self-interest has no place.

Andrew Harvey says that unless we leave our "private" spiritual experiences and "private" concerns and pull together our passion and anger, we will not have been on the spiritual journey at all. Spirituality is not just about being cozy with God, but about allowing yourself to be used by God to make things better in the world.[12]

There is another part to Harvey's message, which is that service is a route to salvation. Harvey does not mean this in the old way of racking up "brownie points," but in terms of transformation. Service dissolves the self. When you want nothing more than to serve all beings, you enter into the timeless dimension of divine love and lose the separate self that is the cause of all suffering.[13]

Christian contemplative Bernadette Roberts says this:

A final and complete loss of self is not achieved by ecstasy, spiritual marriage, or by any such comparable experience, but rather by years of such selfless living that, without satisfaction accruing to the self, the self must die.[14]

Roberts goes on to say, "What makes this selfless giving possible, however, is the self's initial union with God: outside this union, this particular type of giving is not possible."[15] This may

---

12. Andrew Harvey, lecture in Boulder, CO, March 1996.
13. Andrew Harvey, *The Return of the Mother*, p. 266.
14. Bernadette Roberts, *The Path to No-Self* (Boston: Shambhala, 1985), p. 5.
15. Bernadette Roberts, *The Path to No-Self*, p. 5.

seem a bit confusing at first glance. On one hand, she is saying that selfless service is what leads to the dissolution of the ego, yet it is made possible only by the earlier dissolution of the ego in mystical union. I think that experiences of mystical union (almost always brief in terms of clock time) provide a foundation which sustains a life of service, and a life of service frees us from our self-absorption. I would not go so far as Roberts in her assertion that mystical union is the foundation for all service. Some people may have had no experiences of mystical union, and yet adopt service as their path.

The path of service is a path valued in perhaps every religion. The 4th-century Christian hermits, who left the world to live in the desert and seek communion with God, valued charity over everything else. Love and care for one's brother were more important to them than solitude and prayer, than knowledge or contemplation. In the words of Thomas Merton, without love, all these others mean nothing.

With love, Merton said, you see the other as yourself. "We have to become, in some sense, the person we love. And this involves a kind of death of our own being, our own self."[16]

Mahayana Buddhism says much the same thing. The bodhisattva (the eternally selfless giver) feels all pain as his or her own. There is no self and no other, no giver and no receiver. This takes service out of the realm of ego entirely.

Service is a natural outgrowth of spiritual life. It may grow out of the insight into our underlying oneness or come simply as the result of an open and responsive heart. Service is love in action.

---

16. Thomas Merton, *The Wisdom of the Desert: Sayings from the Desert Fathers of the Fourth Century* (Boston: Shambhala, 1994), p. 28.

chapter 14

Riches of the Night

Shining in the darkness
the riches light the way.
Do not remove them.
They belong to the night.

The night is an important image for the mystic. We can learn more about its meaning by considering how night is different from day. Day is our time for the ordinary activities of life. It is our time for getting things done. The self is in charge, and the mind is active. Day thus represents ordinary life and ordinary consciousness.

Night, in contrast, is the time we become passive and receptive. When we lie helpless in our sleep, our dreams come to us. The night also provides an opportunity to develop our other faculties. In the physical world, the darkness of night does not allow us to navigate by our dominant sense of vision and we are forced to utilize other senses. In spiritual life, there is what is called the "dark night of the senses" and the "dark night of the spirit (or soul)." These are times when we can no longer know God through the mind and the senses. God has withdrawn from our perception in order to wean us away from these traditional ways of knowing. This serves the goal of contemplative life, which is to draw us into deeper contact with the extraordinary riches of Being that go far, far beyond what the mind and senses can perceive.

These riches are mined in stillness. We discover them, not so much by active pursuit, but by allowing ourselves to disap-

pear into silence. In more mystical language, we lie down with
the Beloved and become one.

MYSTICAL UNION

Mystical union is this absorption into oneness. To reach it, the
soul must be emptied of every obstacle that would separate it
from the Beloved. Only when we are naked and unprotected are
we available for the most intimate contact. The following poem
uses the metaphor of lovers to describe this.

The Beloved Comes

The Beloved comes
when the night has grown still
and all other loves have departed.

I must not search with my eyes
but rather feel with my body,
my heart the most sensitive
to the divine caress.

I wait for a touch so light
it would go unnoticed,
yet placing no barrier
I feel and absorb it completely,
turning ever-so-slightly
into our union.

We melt.
One great *Sea of Being.*
No longer separate,
I am one with All.

Afterwards, I sleep,
my beloved slipping quietly away.

riches of the night

I awaken to find myself deserted,
the emptiness stark and horrifying
until I remember
night will come again.[1]

This poem is rich in metaphoric meaning, and I would like to explain some of its symbolism.

The Beloved comes
when the night has grown still
and all other loves have departed

In the first verse we learn two important things. One is that the Beloved comes in the night which I have described as a state of unknowing. This is very important. Only when we have let go of our minds, can we encounter that which is beyond mind. The other thing I would point out is that the lover lies alone, waiting. We have let go of our other attachments to be really free and available.

I must not search with my eyes
but rather feel with my body,
my heart the most sensitive
to the divine caress.

The eyes represent the conscious mind. The conscious mind is simply not equipped to know God, so we must let go of searching in this way. We can feel the inner nature of Being more easily through the subtle senses and through our bodies. I feel the divine most easily through my heart.

---

1. Jasmin Cori, *Freefall to the Beloved: Mystical Poetry for God's Lovers* (Boulder, CO: Golden Reed, 1996), p. 28.

I wait for a touch so light
it would go unnoticed,
yet placing no barrier
I feel and absorb it completely,
turning ever-so-slightly
into our union.

Here we learn what several have said before: that the perception
of Being is subtle and can go unnoticed if we are not paying
close attention. We feel it only when we put up no barrier; we
must give ourselves completely. In the poem, the lover does this
in a soft way, minimizing her own will.

We melt.
One great Sea of Being.
No longer separate,
I am one with All.

This, of course, is the mystical experience of oneness. It is the
erasure of all separation and of self.

Afterwards, I sleep,
my beloved slipping quietly away.
I awaken to find myself deserted,
the emptiness stark and horrifying
until I remember
night will come again.

Rarely can we maintain mystical consciousness for long. We fall
back asleep, returning to ordinary consciousness and the
activities of daily life. Having tasted union, we now feel its
absence more keenly. Our only consolation is in remembering
that night will come again. Notice that, in the poem, I do not
say that the Beloved will come again. But the requisite condi-

tions of consciousness will return and there is the hope of the Beloved returning as well. It is this possibility that we cultivate by living a contemplative life.

On the Way to the Beloved

Just as the experience of sexual union is usually preceded by foreplay, union with the divine is preceded by pleasurable contact. In this case, it is contact with our own essential nature, the divine nature in which we participate. The spiritual journey is one of coming to know this nature. It is a journey full of surprises, a progressive unveiling of something infinitely beautiful.

This progressive unveiling reminds me of an experience I had when I moved from the Midwest to Grand Junction, Colorado. Grand Junction is a small town butting up against the Colorado National Monument. If you have never been there or seen pictures of it, the Colorado National Monument is a large area of land with huge sandstone walls sculpted and painted by the elements. In my first forays there, I drove up perhaps a mile, got out of my car, and hung out there, marveling at the beauty. Each time I went up, I drove a little farther, and each time I was amazed that there could be yet more of this treasure. I think I had lived there for six months before I drove with a friend across the length of the monument, which is a little over twenty miles. I laughed to discover how little I had actually seen, even though I had been in the park many, many times. In retrospect, I am glad I experienced it in little chunks as I did. Each venture had been absolutely rich and full.

I had a similar experience working in my spiritual school. I was fortunate to pick an approach that felt like taking a detailed tour of the inner dimensions. Each new state of consciousness was an incredible adventure. Each was a marvel. There seemed to be an endless variety of possibilities.

Particularly at first, our experiences are clothed in imagery the mind can relate to. We tap the alphabet of the familiar in order to bring the unfamiliar into range. Let me give you an example. As I was meeting aspects of myself that I had not consciously met before, I first experienced these through visual and kinesthetic images that best approximated them. For example, when I was feeling a very delicate, vulnerable kind of love, I would often experience myself as a sweet flower. When I was experiencing a fierce protective energy, I became a tiger. Sometimes the images were quite whimsical. They grew out of something I was meeting inside, but the mind clothed them in its own imaginative ways, as you'll see in the following experience.

This incident occurred during a time when I was distressed because my life had veered so far away from any path I could recognize. I felt no security, no stability, no sense of how I fit into the world. I was working with a teacher who had me tune into my body. I felt something protruding out from my belly center, an energy that provided some kind of support. The protrusion grew, until I found myself riding in a boat. I called it my "moon boat," because it was shaped like a crescent moon. I was paddling among the stars, a setting rich in symbolic meaning for me. My teacher had once told me that our essence is so rich and has so many aspects that there are more ways we can experience it than there are stars in the sky. I felt that this moon boat was taking me on the greatest adventure possible, and I was as happy as I could be.

Like dream images, experiences like these reflect inner states and can serve as pointers to the transpersonal dimensions. I would like to share two other images that came in a workshop with Sufi teacher Atum Thomas O'Kane. The first came during an exercise in which we were invited to feel the divine impulse within us. As I went inside myself, I felt as if I were reaching deep into the earth, like the roots of a tree. I felt the roots first, and then the branches spreading out wide. The tree was in blossom so the branches were covered with flowers. After a moment, this tree began to sing. It was not that the tree was making up a song of its own; it was singing the song of the earth. In other words, the earth was singing through the tree. Atum called this a "living image." He suggested that I stay with it, because it had things to teach me. Some of those lessons are readily apparent. I have a vivid sense of letting something larger express itself through my writing.

This was confirmed in a second living image, this time of the inner teacher. As we were guided inward, I experienced myself as the inside of an earthen well. Many voices from various traditions could be heard in this well. I wondered for a moment if I needed to mediate between them or somehow select some over others. Then I saw that the voices were drawn through a heart at the top of the well. They moved through this heart and became birds, flying in many directions. I think you can see the theme common to these two experiences. It is not the language (the image) itself that is important, but the living reality that gives rise to it. The experiences are just a reflection of this.

I also had to learn to let images and experiences arise without feeling the need to make sense of them. I remember once feeling as if it were raining flowers all around me. I never did understand that image, but it doesn't matter. What is important is to allow the experience to unfold. What it is leading us to is more important than the phenomena we encounter along the way.

We must keep a delicate balance. It is useful to pay attention to our experience, but it isn't helpful to cling to it. Spiritual teacher Hameed Ali (A. H. Almaas of The Diamond Approach)

once said that spiritual experiences are like a light show generated as the ego dissolves. They are the product of consciousness
"discharging." They are what happen on the way to reality.

This brings us back to what Tibetan Buddhist teacher
Chögyam Trungpa said about spiritual materialism. Our ego
likes to collect spiritual experiences and use them to inflate
itself. It reminds me of the trapped animal that can't get free
because it won't let go of the bait. If we hold on to our experiences in a way that bolsters the ego, we harden our structure
and we become further distanced from true nature.

There is a paradox here. Our spiritual experiences feel
incredibly deep and personal, intimate and real—and they are,
because they are experiences of our deeper nature. Yet these
same experiences that feel so piercingly intimate are still the
outer layer of something so interior that the mind cannot reach
it. What the mind cannot reach, we cannot articulate.

Let us return to the opening verse of this chapter, which
tells us not to try to remove the riches; they belong to the night.
Our deepest experiences in contemplation happen when the
mind is still. Those experiences that do waft up through the
silence and touch the mind must be treated with care. To try to
make them into routines and affirmations may put them into an
unnatural form and trivialize what is so much deeper. We must
let contemplative life disappear into the night and honor the
mystery that it is.

Bibliography

Almaas, A. H. *Diamond Heart, Book One.* Berkeley: Diamond Books, 1987.

Ban Breathnach, Sarah. *Simple Abundance: A Daybook for Comfort and Joy.* New York: Warner, 1995.

Beck, Charlotte Joko. *Everyday Zen: Love and Work.* San Francisco: HarperSanFrancisco, 1989.

———. *Nothing Special: Living Zen.* San Francisco: HarperSanFrancisco, 1993.

Brother Lawrence. *The Practice of the Presence of God.* New York: Doubleday, 1977.

Cori, Jasmin Lee. *Freefall to the Beloved: Mystical Poetry for God's Lovers.* Boulder, CO: Golden Reed, 1996.

Easwaran, Eknath. *Blue Mountain: A Journal for Spiritual Living.* New York: Seabury Press, 1981.

Elgin, Duane. *Voluntary Simplicity: Toward a Way of Life that Is Outwardly, Simple, Inwardly Rich.* New York: William Morrow, 1993.

Hanh, Thich Nhat. *For a Future to Be Possible.* Berkeley: Parallax Press, 1993.

Harvey, Andrew. *The Return of the Mother.* Berkeley: Frog, Ltd., 1995.

Keating, Father Thomas. *Open Mind, Open Heart: The Contemplative Dimension.* New York: Continuum Publishing, 1995.

Khan, Hazrat Inayat. *The Art of Personality.* The Sufi Message Series, vol. VIII. Delhi: Motilal Banarsidass, 1989/1996.

Matousek, Mark. "Should You Design Your Own Religion?", *Utne Reader,* July–August 1998.

May, Gerald D. *The Awakening Heart: Opening Yourself to the Love You Need.* San Francisco: HarperSanFrancisco, 1991.

Merton, Thomas. *Thoughts in Solitude.* Boston: Shambhala, 1993.

———. *The Wisdom of the Desert: Sayings from the Desert Fathers of the Fourth Century.* Boston: Shambhala, 1994.

Moore, Thomas. *Meditations on the Monk Who Dwells in Daily Life*. New York: HarperCollins, 1994.

Mother Theresa, and Lucina Vardy, ed. *A Simple Path*. New York: Ballantine, 1995.

Packer, Toni. *The Light of Discovery*. Boston: Tuttle, 1995.

————. *The Work of This Moment*. Boston: Shambhala, 1990.

Pierrako, Eva. *The Pathwork of Self-Transformation*. New York: Bantam, 1990.

Progoff, Ira. *The Well and the Cathedral*. New York: Dialogue House Library, 1977.

Roberts, Bernadette. *The Experience of No-Self*. Boston: Shambhala, 1993.

————. *The Path to No-Self*. Boston: Shambhala, 1991.

St. James, Elaine. *Living the Simple Life*. New York: Hyperion, 1996.

Toms, Michael. *At the Leading Edge*. Burdette, NY: Larson Publications, 1990.

Trungpa, Chögyam. *Cutting Through Spiritual Materialism*. Boston: Shambhala, 1987.

Tweedie, Irena. *Daughter of Fire: A Diary of a Spiritual Training with a Sufi Master*. Inverness, CA: Golden Sufi Center, 1986.

VandenBroeck, Goldian, ed. *Less Is More: The Art of Voluntary Poverty*. Rochester, VT: Inner Traditions, 1978.

Vaughan-Lee, Llewellyn. *The Call and the Echo*. Putney, VT: Threshold Books, 1992.

————. *In the Company of Friends*. Inverness, CA: Golden Sufi Center, 1994.

Welwood, John. *Journey of the Heart: Intimate Relationship and the Path to Love*. New York: Harper Perennial, 1990.

————. *Love and Awakening: Discovering the Sacred Path of Intimate Relationship*. New York: HarperCollins, 1996.

Suggested Reading List

Almaas, A. H. *Diamond Heart Book One: Elements of the Real in Man.* Berkeley:
Diamond Books, 1987.

———. *Diamond Heart Book Two: The Freedom to Be.* Berkeley: Diamond
Books, 1989.

———. *Diamond Heart Book Three: Being and the Meaning of Life.* Berkeley:
Diamond Books, 1990.

———. *Diamond Heart Book Four: Indestructible Innocence.* Berkeley:
Diamond Books, 1997.

———. *Essence* with *The Elixir of Enlightenment* (Two Books in One
Volume). York Beach, ME: Samuel Weiser, 1998.

Baldwin, Christina. *Life's Companion: Journal Writing as a Spiritual Quest.*
New York: Bantam, 1991.

Beck, Charlotte Joko. *Everyday Zen.* San Francisco: HarperSanFrancisco,
1989.

———. *Nothing Special: Living Zen.* San Francisco: HarperSanFrancisco,
1993.

Brother Lawrence. *The Practice of the Presence of God.* Pomfret, VT:
Trafalgar Square, 1997.

Cooper, David A. *Heart of Stillness: The Elements of Spiritual Practice.* New
York: Bell Tower, 1992.

Elgin, Duane. *Voluntary Simplicity: Toward a Way of Life that is Outwardly
Simple, Inwardly Rich.* New York: William Morrow, 1993.

Godman, David, ed. *Be as You Are: The Teachings of Sri Ramana Maharshi.*
London: Arkana, 1985.

Groeschel, Benedict J. *Spiritual Passages: The Psychology of Spiritual
Development.* New York: Crossroad, 1983.

Hanh, Thich Nhat. *Living Buddha, Living Christ.* New York: Riverhead
Books, 1995.

suggested reading list

———. *Peace Is Every Step: The Path of Mindfulness in Everyday Life*. New York: Bantam, 1991.

Harrison, Gavin. *In the Lap of the Buddha*. Boston: Shambhala, 1994.

Harvey, Andrew. *The Return of the Mother*. Berkeley: Frog, 1995.

Hixon, Lex. *Coming Home: The Experience of Enlightenment in Sacred Traditions*. Los Angeles: J. P. Tarcher, 1978.

Huff, Benjamin. *The Tao of Pooh*. New York: E. P. Dutton., 1982.

Keating, Father Thomas. *Open Mind, Open Heart: The Contemplative Dimension of the Gospel*. New York: Continnuum, 1995.

Kornfield, Jack. *A Path with Heart*. New York: Bantam, 1993.

Levine, Stephen. *A Gradual Awakening*. New York: Doubleday, 1979.

May, Gerald G. *The Awakened Heart: Opening Yourself to the Love You Need*. San Francisco: HarperSanFrancisco, 1991.

Ming-Dao, Deng. *Everyday Tao: Living with Balance and Harmony*. San Francisco: HarperSanFrancisco, 1996.

Muller, Wayne. *Sabbath: Restoring the Sacred Rhythm of Rest*. New York: Bantam, 1999.

Packer, Toni. *The Light of Discovery*. Boston: Tuttle, 1995.

Roberts, Bernadette. *The Experience of No-Self*. Shambhala, 1985.

———. *The Path to No-Self*. Shambhala, 1985.

Sinetar, Marsha. *Ordinary People as Monks and Mystics*. Mahwah, NJ: Paulist Press, 1986.

Thesenga, Susan. *The Undefended Self: Living the Pathwork of Spiritual Wholeness*. Del Mar, CA: Pathwork Press, 1994.

Vaughan-Lee, Llwellyn. *The Bond with the Beloved*. Inverness, CA: The Golden Sufi Center, 1993.

———. *The Call & the Echo*. Putney, VT: Threshold Books, 1992.

———. *In the Company of Friends*. Inverness, CA: Golden Sufi Center, 1994.

———. *Paradoxes of Love*. Inverness, CA: Golden Sufi Center, 1996.

Welwood, John. *Journey of the Heart: Intimate Relationship and the Path of Love*. New York: HarperCollins, 1990.

———. *Love & Awakening: Discovering the Sacred Path of Intimate Relationship*. New York: HarperCollins, 1996.

———. *Ordinary Magic: Everyday Life as Spiritual Path*. Boston: Shambhala, 1992.

Index

A

abundance, 29, 32
    misunderstanding of, 31
addiction, 39
Almaas, A. H., 45, 52, 103, 123
alone, being, 48
appreciation, 114
attachments, 52, 89
aversion and desire, 64

B

balance, 10
Beck, Charlotte Joko, 87, 114
Being, 9, 94, 97, 101, 111, 120
    flow of, 111
    pure, 73
    reality of, 49
    simplicity of, 26
    true, 5
Beloved, 64, 106, 110, 118, 119
    giving yourself to the, 6
    on the way to the, 121
beneath the surface, 99
birds
    soaring, 53
    two, 53
Bonaventura, Saint, 30
Breathnach, Sarah Ban, 28
Brother, Lawrence, 108

C

Chögyam Trungpa, 14, 15, 124
Chuang Tzu, 10
clutter, 25, 28
codependency, 52
concentration, 57
consciousness, 73, 80
    mystical, 120
    prosperity, 31
contemplation, 6, 67, 77
    the natural way, 9, 17
control, 90
Cosmic Consciousness, 86
current, the, 94

D

Dances of Universal Peace, 109
dependency, judging, 84
detachment, 42, 43
dhikr, 108, 109
Diamond Approach, 123
discernment, 12, 14
Divine Mother, 110
divine, union with, 121
Don Juan, Yaqui sorcerer, 111
dream images, 122

index

index

Jasmin Lee Cori is a licensed psychotherapist in private practice who uses a transpersonal approach to help people live from a deeper place. She earned her undergraduate degree at Central Michigan University and holds a Masters in Clinical Psychology from Indiana State University. After ten years of teaching psychology and personal growth classes in a number of colleges and professional programs, she now turns her attention to spiritual work and writing.

Jasmin's spiritual training includes the modern spiritual teaching known as The Diamond Approach, as well as a number of major traditions. She shares the Taoist's love for the spontaneous and natural, and the Sufi's emphasis on love for the Beloved. At this point, she is no longer following a common path, but rather following the truth wherever that leads her. She has also written *Freefall to the Beloved: Mystical Poetry for God's Lovers* and the forthcoming *Trust Walk: A Journey of Awakening.* Currently she makes her home in Boulder, CO.